Bringing Jamie Home Trilogy

Part One

Jamie's Choice

Also by Sherile Reilly

Historical Paranormal Romance

Lord of Darkness

Contemporary Romance

Bringing Jamie Home Trilogy:
Jamie's Choice
Jamie's Secret
Jamie's Gift

Children's Books

Greg and the Barbarian
Spunky: Tapping into Trouble

Bringing Jamie Home Trilogy

Part One

Jamie's Choice

Sherile Reilly

ISBN 978-0-9879942-5-7

Publisher: Saborn Press
Cover Design: Lorraine Paton
Print Cover Design: April Martinez

Second Edition

www.SherileReilly.com

Dedication and Acknowledgments

For Ed, with love…

Thanks to all the people who have helped with this book:
Lorraine Paton, Catherine Saykaly-Stevens, Adrienne Kerr,
Ted Williams, Donna Tunney, Suzanne Stengl, Brenda
Collins and Betty Bruerton.

Chapter One

It was a perfect spring morning—until I looked out my living room window. The ten-year-old monster from across the street was squatting in front of my flowerbed—with his left hand strangling three of my prize-winning red tulips and his right hand wielding a pair of scissors.

I rapped on the windowpane and yelled, "Stop!"

You'd think the kid was an Olympic sprinter and I'd fired the gun. He exploded into action, scooping up red and yellow tulips from the sidewalk, lowering his head, and darting across the street. By the time I got to the front door, he was disappearing around the side of his house and I was left standing there, surrounded by the smell of something burning.

Despite my outrage, it wasn't me. It was the meat in the oven.

I raced into the kitchen, turned off the stove, and opened the oven door. Heat blasted my face and I backed up. I should have known better, because the fan was blowing and the oven was still at 375 degrees. I wasn't thinking about roast beef dinners, though. I kept seeing the painful image of my beautiful tulips, lying like fallen sentinels, on the walkway outside my door.

I shook my head, thinking: *Didn't the little kid's mother teach him the difference between right and wrong?* I'd have a talk with her, but first I had to attend to the meal I'd promised

Dottie—the widow who lives next door.

Since I moved into the neighborhood, I've taken Dottie one or two suppers a week. Today I was doing supper at lunch time, so I could work all afternoon and evening on my renovation and interior design presentation.

It didn't take me long to slice the roast. I put the browned end pieces on a plate and covered them with aluminum foil. I liked to keep the meat as hot as possible for Dottie. She had lived in the neighborhood for decades and was the only person who had been really friendly to me since I moved in, over a year ago.

Ten minutes later, I stood on Dottie's doorstep and raised my hand to ring the bell. I didn't get the chance. Dottie opened the door first—a big grin on her face.

"I brought your favorite roast-beef dinner," I said, passing the bag to her and avoiding her soul-searching gaze. I had work to do and didn't want to get trapped into visiting with Dottie while she ate.

I should have known I couldn't get away quickly.

"Let's have a visit," she said, taking the brown paper bag out of my hand and motioning for me to come in.

"Not today. I've got an errand I want to finish up." I gave her a brave smile, knowing full well that if I ever let Dottie know what I was going to do, she would have all sorts of advice for me. As it was, she couldn't let me get away without asking her favorite question.

"An errand?" She sighed. "When is a nice girl like you going to get a husband?" Her eyes gleamed and opened wider, as if expecting me to divulge some juicy revelation about my love life.

It was non-existent. It hadn't existed for … well, I didn't want to remember how long. The first time she'd asked this question, I had foolishly obliged her with a detailed answer. I explained about renovations and establishing my business—McGivney's Renovations and

Design—a full-time job. I also explained that I liked being a singleton.

Dottie's eyes had widened and her mouth dropped open. "Don't belittle your state, Rachel. You're *not* a simpleton and don't *ever* call yourself that!"

Surprised, I had replied, "I said sin-gle-ton," carefully enunciating each syllable, so that Dottie would understand the joke.

She had put her fists on her hips, showing her defiance. "That is not a word."

Being from an older generation, Dottie hadn't understood, and after more than a year of conversations, she was still trying to fix my love life. She shook her finger at me. "You're not getting any younger, Rachel McGivney. All the good prospects will be snatched up before you know it, and you'll be a spinster all your life. You don't want that."

The word spinster conjured up visions of my piano teacher with her hair in a bun, a printed black dress with wide lapels, and heavy black shoes. I could remember sitting on the piano bench when I was a kid and wondering if my teacher was a witch in disguise. I always hoped I wouldn't be her next victim.

Did the child across the street think I was a witch?

I patted Dottie's hand, ready to say goodbye.

She raised her eyebrows. "It's Friday. Do you at least have a date for tonight?"

"Not tonight."

She scrutinized me. "Why do you have your beautiful dark hair pulled back so severely? It makes you look stern."

"It's convenient and doesn't get in my face."

"You'd be a very fetching woman if you allowed yourself to get out of those matronly clothes. In that outfit, you look like an undertaker. Oh, my." Dottie shook her head and let out a big sigh. "What am I going to do with you?"

I tried not to be offended by her scathing appraisal. I had always considered black pants and a turtleneck to be good business attire. With a jacket completing my outfit, I was comfortable meeting with my clients.

Dottie's expression changed from skeptical to hopeful. "I know," she said, answering her own question. "I'll go shopping with you ... anytime you want. Together, we could make you sophisticated and sexy."

"Sure. We'll do that sometime," I replied, without any conviction in my voice.

She waggled her finger at me. "I know the brush-off when I hear it, but think about what I've said, Rachel. That long, dark hair of yours is lovely, and those brown eyes could melt any man's heart."

I backed down the stairs, hoping that today's assessment was complete, but she just couldn't let me get away without one last bit of advice.

"You don't have too many pretty years left, Rachel, and a good man is hard to come by. Don't wait too long."

Dottie was in fine form today—undeterred by my obvious attempts at retreat—peppering me with prying questions and making it sound as though my shelf life was about to expire. At thirty-eight, I liked to think the field was still wide open, but when I was being truthful with myself, I had to admit that the town of Maryville is really just a bedroom community and doesn't have a large singles population. However, with all the new housing going up, it's great for my interior design and decorating business. Homeowners with two incomes and no kids love to have show-home decor, and I'm pleased to offer my skills.

I diverted Dottie's interest from my lackluster love life. "I've got another job, so I'm going to be busy tonight."

"Good for you. Don't worry though, I'll keep my eyes and ears open for an eligible bachelor." She winked and nodded as if we were co-conspirators.

"You do that, Dottie." I waved and walked up the street, determined, but cringing at the thought of my next job—talking to the monster's mother.

Chapter Two

I stood on the sidewalk, studying the house. I'd seen an older man come to the place on a few occasions, usually at the beginning of the month, but he never stayed for long so I assumed he was the landlord. Although the yard was tidy and the lawn always mowed, there hadn't been any upgrades made to the 1950s bungalow. I wondered if the landlord was hoping to sell to a developer. The neighborhood was changing, with the older houses being demolished and luxury homes replacing them.

I climbed the front steps and rang the bell. While I waited, I noticed that the vinyl siding needed washing, and the cement steps were crumbling at the edges. I glanced across the street to my house. I liked the changes I'd made: pristine white stucco and a newly painted iron railing. It was a huge improvement from the house in which my mother and I had lived.

Hinges squeaked behind me and I turned—standing tall—ready to make my case for the return of the stolen tulips.

Mrs. Sorenson, about whom I knew very little, opened the inside door and nodded at me through the screen, not seeming particularly surprised by my presence.

She looked tired and pale, and her hair was thin and limp. I'd seen her before from my living room window and she'd been walking along the street, carrying groceries.

She'd glanced up, smiled, and waved—seeming to be a gentle soul. A big lump filled my throat. I really hated what I was going to do, but I soldiered on, determined that the boy wouldn't get away with his bad behavior.

"Please, come in," she said, gesturing me toward the living room as if I were an honored guest. She followed me. "I don't think we've ever been properly introduced." She stuck out her hand. "Elena Sorenson."

"Rachel McGivney. Nice to meet you."

We shook hands and then she indicated the sofa. "Would you like to have a seat?"

I sat down facing a huge picture window, through which I could see my house. Mrs. Sorenson sat in an overstuffed armchair on the other side of the room. Beside her, on a small, round table, was a vase of flowers.

My red and yellow tulips. I swallowed, knowing that their beauty was short-lived once they were cut.

I wanted to get on with the conversation regarding her son, but she gazed at my tulips as if they were the first and most beautiful bouquet she'd ever received. I didn't have the heart to begin discussing the theft.

I noticed a piece of battered cardboard leaning against the vase. I could just make out the words:

To Mommy
Love Jamie

So he'd given the flowers to his mom. From the look in her eye, I could tell that she loved them. *So who am I to rain on her parade?*

"I'm so glad you came to visit me today. I've wanted to talk to you, but ..." She pinched her lips and blinked. For a moment, I thought she was going to cry, but then she straightened her spine, pulled back her shoulders, and seemed to fight for control. "I've admired the work you do in your yard, and heard good things about you at the grocery store." The words came out in a rush, sounding like a prepared speech.

I wasn't impressed with the grocery store recommendation, but I found my anger dwindling, replaced by empathy. I wondered whether she worked, and how she could even hold a job with such a worn-out look. *Who wouldn't be tired raising a badly mannered child?* I also couldn't forget the kid's big, stupid sheepdog, who had absolutely no sense of where to do his business. For him, anyone's well-manicured lawn was a target. This spring, I'd seen the evidence of his doggy doo and piddle power: circles of dead, yellow grass surrounded by clumps of unruly green. It'd brought back memories of the sour odor that had filled the mobile home Mom and I moved into, after the tragedy. The broadloom was stained, and the closed-up space reeked of dog poop. We'd scrubbed and sanitized everything, but long after the stench was gone, I never forgot.

Mrs. Sorenson looked at the tulips again, and then sighed, giving me a weary gaze that made it clear she was aware of their origin. "Jamie likes to give me gifts," she said, apologetically.

And his dumb dog likes to give me *gifts*, I thought, but held my tongue.

Mrs. Sorenson continued before I could think of a more diplomatic response. "Jamie doesn't always do the right thing, but his heart is in the right place and he really is a good boy."

She gave another love-struck look at the tulips, and before I could stop myself, I waved my hand dismissively and struggled against the sudden thickness in my throat. "It's okay. They're only flowers."

Even if they *were* the ones I had planned to cut tomorrow, and enter in the horticultural society's annual spring show and competition. Last spring, I'd been a newcomer to town and had won the prize for the best flower in show. In the fall, I'd worked really hard on my flowerbeds, separating the bulbs and replanting them— confident that I had a good chance at winning the big prize this spring. Now my only chance was sitting in a vase, and I felt like a big meanie for even caring. *Who could snatch happiness away from an exhausted mother?*

"You're so kind and considerate."

She wouldn't say that if she knew what I was thinking about her kid just a few minutes ago.

"I want Jamie to make amends for what he did." She placed her hand on the end table and gazed lovingly at the tulips. "I've explained to him that what he did was not right, and that he has to help you."

"Help me what?" The big lump in my throat almost choked me. I didn't like where this conversation was heading.

"Jamie has said he would like to assist you with the gardening. He's willing to help you with the tulips."

He had already helped himself *to* my tulips. What else did he want to do to my poor flowers? Dig them up? "I don't think that's necessary." I tried to keep my voice calm and offer a gracious smile, but was afraid it probably looked more like a grimace.

She slumped a bit in her chair. It was terrible. I had the impression I'd made a major faux pas. I didn't know what it was, but it felt as if I'd kicked all her dreams into the garbage pail. *Okay,* I thought, *maybe she thinks having Jamie digging alongside me in the flowerbeds will be therapeutic or ... whatever.* I had the dreadful feeling that I'd be the one getting punished.

"You'll find he's a caring, sensitive boy who just wants to be loved." Her expression looked dreamy and preoccupied.

I didn't trust myself to make any comments about her beloved Jamie. He wasn't my kid, and I didn't really care for his company. I knew that little boys could look like angels, but cause terrible heartache. I was just thankful that I didn't have to raise him. My conscience gave me a big kick, and the next thing I knew, I was nodding like one of those silly, little bobble-head dolls and spewing calming words.

"If it's okay with you, Jamie can come over tomorrow and work with me for two hours. Can he start at nine?" I managed to keep my tone pleasant. I figured I'd get my punishment over with early in the morning, so the rest of the day would be mine.

"You're wonderful." She clapped her hands, as if she'd won the lottery. "I want to ask a favor of you." Her eyes brightened. "I'm having a special party next Friday night and I'd love for you to come. I've invited a few of the neighbors. I'm calling it my 'Under the Mistletoe Party' because this year I'm celebrating Christmas early."

I wondered why anyone would want to celebrate Christmas before we'd even had summer. I'd check with Dottie and find out what was going on.

I hated mistletoe. In high school, I'd been invited to a few Christmas parties and there was always mistletoe. To the hordes of testosterone-fueled high school boys, it was the perfect opportunity for giving me wet, invasive kisses, while they gripped me with one hand and pawed me with the other. Since my mother and I lived on the wrong side of the tracks, I was considered trailer trash and presumably available. I discovered that if I always had my nose in a book, I stopped getting invited to such parties, allowing me to avoid confrontations. I didn't want to fantasize about boys or imagine how it would feel to be kissed by one I liked, so I avoided any contact with them.

I realized I'd been allowing my thoughts to wander, so I hastily said, "It's very kind of you to invite me. Thank you."

. . . . .

After the meeting with Elena, I'd driven to my latest project and met with Cory, my site manager.

Starting in his late teens, he'd worked in the construction industry for twenty years and knew about everything from wiring to plumbing. On site I'd appreciated his work ethic and knowledge. His good sense of team work with the men and his ability to see the project through to the finished product made him the ideal contractor.

After we'd discussed the work in progress, I left and was looking forward to some quiet time at home.

I was cruising down my front street when a boy on a bicycle darted out from between two parked cars. I swerved and failed to notice the big, white sheepdog a few feet behind him.

I jammed on my brakes. Tires screeched. I jerked forward, my seat belt tightening across my chest.

The kid, who I realized was Jamie, had gotten off his bike. Kneeling, and with his arms around the dog's neck, he said, "Did she hurt you? Are you okay, boy?"

Jamie stood and glared at me, like I'd deliberately tried to run down his dog.

The dog's rear end wiggled, reminding me of a hula dance and at the same time, assuring me that he was not injured.

I leaned out the car window and raised my arm. "I wasn't trying to hurt your dog, but if the two of you keep running into the street either you or your dog could get killed."

"His name's Scooter." Jamie's lower lip pushed out.

Realizing I'd been shaking my fist at a child and guilty of behaving like one myself, I dropped my hand to my lap, determined to regain my self-control. I took a breath before

I said, "You need to get your dog under control."

Ignoring my words, he gazed at his house and then at the sky, appearing to forget me and my advice. I glared at him, wanting him to understand, but before I could think of anything to say, he got on his bicycle and raced down the street with the dog behind him.

My stomach ached. Maybe I'd been a bit forceful in scolding him. When would he learn?

Chapter Three

On Saturday morning, I ripped weeds out of the overgrown front flowerbed. I'd put Jamie and the tulip theft behind me and reminded myself that winning the best flower in the horticultural show last spring was really a fluke. The tulips had been planted long before I'd bought the house and I really couldn't take credit for their marvelous blooms.

Today, I had a new target—the weedy flowerbed on the left side of the front steps. This would be my first chance to get it ready for the bedding out plants. I'd always loved the brightness of red geraniums, and in a few weeks, I'd buy the potted plants. They'd make a beautiful display when I planted them in early June. I remembered saving enough money to buy a single pot of purple and white pansies when I was ten. They'd bloomed all summer and I'd given each friendly pansy a name. I loved those flowers.

I decided that if Jamie showed up, I'd let him work in the backyard. There was a long-neglected flowerbed along the back fence. He could dig at the weeds as long as he wanted and couldn't hurt anything. My recently purchased flowerpots, with their display of yellow daffodils and purple hyacinths, were on the cement patio near the foundation. Jamie didn't have to go anywhere near them.

"Good morning, Rachel."

Startled, I looked up. Mrs. Sorenson had Jamie by the

hand, as if she were afraid he might bolt if she let go. He had a box in his right hand. His head was down and his shoulders slumped.

I felt like she was handing over a prisoner—and I was the new warden.

"I'm pleased you brought Jamie over." I stared at the kid. We had one thing in common: our mutual dislike of each other.

"Jamie's brought a treat for both of you to enjoy later." Elena nudged him toward me.

Like a robot, he thrust the cardboard box at me. I pulled off my gloves and accepted it. "Thank you. Both of you," I added.

Mrs. Sorenson's expression brightened. "I've also brought some lemonade." She opened the white cotton bag she'd been carrying over her left arm.

I noticed that her skin was almost as pale as the bag. She pulled out a plastic jug filled with lemonade. Two paper cups were resting upside-down over the lid.

I wondered if she thought I'd let her kid die of thirst. She was making all the peace offerings—overdoing it in my opinion. Wanting to speed the job along, I said, "Okay, Jamie, it's time for you to get to work."

I took the container she offered me. "I'll bring Jamie home in two hours."

She touched my arm. "Thanks, Rachel. You working with my son gives me such a good feeling." She placed her hand over her heart, making me feel as if I didn't have one. Her dress and sweater hung loosely from her shoulders. In the next moment, she pressed her left hand against her temple and covered her mouth with her other hand, stifling a gasp. She twitched and I grasped her elbow, supporting her.

"Are you all right?"

She wiped the sweat from her forehead. "I'll be okay."

She took a deep breath and shivered. Then she patted Jamie on the head. "Mind what I've told you and be a good boy for Rachel."

She ruffled his hair and smiled as if he were the only child in the world. "I'll leave you two to get better acquainted." Without another word, she crossed the street and I saw Jamie watching her with gut-wrenching grief in his eyes—his mouth twisted in pain.

I know I'm not the best with kids. I'd proved that years ago, but Jamie's expression made me feel really cruel. He didn't have to say anything or even look at me. Coldness reached out from his body and his sorrow hit me like a knife slashing my skin, exposing it to the cruelties of the world.

I shook myself, dispelling my dark ideas.

"Follow me, young man. It's time for us to get to work."

He shrugged and shuffled along behind me as I led the way around the side of the house, under the white wooden trellis, and into the backyard. I stopped and surveyed my domain, still proud of my first home purchase. I'd scrimped and saved for the down payment, and when I bought the house last spring, I'd had a new cement patio poured and a new six-foot-high, cinder-block fence constructed, complete with a top row of decorative bricks. To the right of the house was a single garage. The former owner had left it loaded with broken equipment, shelves of tools, jars of nails, and sheets of old, dark wall paneling. There was no room for my car, and after I'd taken possession, I'd closed the garage and hadn't looked inside again. Cleanup would come later. This summer would see the completion of the backyard and the second front flowerbed.

"Jamie, you'll work over there." I pointed to the back of the lot, trying to infuse enthusiasm into my voice. "I'll show you what to do." I took a hand cultivator and a pair of gloves from the patio table and handed them to Jamie. He looked at them as if I'd handed him little green aliens.

"I bought the gloves for you. They'll fit."

He scrutinized me, his eyes big and full of sorrow.

The kid really knew how to play the little innocent, but I wouldn't allow myself to be fooled by his woeful expression.

"The sooner we start this job, the sooner we'll be finished." I don't know what possessed me to say "we." Where Jamie was concerned, I wanted as little "we" as possible.

I knelt on the grass at the edge of the weed-infested flowerbed and pointed to the small cotoneaster saplings that were valiantly struggling to survive. "I'm going to keep all of these plants. You can pull out or dig up the rest." I yanked at a weed entangling the cotoneaster and threw it in the rubbish box. "Go ahead and I'll check your progress in half an hour."

Before I rounded the corner, I glanced back at him. Jamie was on his knees with his head bent low. I convinced myself that a couple of hours of yard work would be good for him. He was safe and I'd enjoy my uninterrupted gardening time, far away from him.

In a few minutes, I was digging at the scraggly pieces of grass that were creeping into the flowerbed I'd neglected last summer. It was in the shade of a twenty-foot blue spruce on the opposite side of the walkway from my tulips. I loved the evergreen, with its soft new growth. After edging the flowerbed, I cultivated around a thriving juniper. I credited the shade for its lush foliage. With a little TLC, I'd have this flowerbed finished in no time. I leaned over and picked up clumps of sod, knocked the dirt from the roots, and threw them into a box for recycling.

I hadn't been working long when I heard a dog yapping. I looked around, but couldn't see one. I bent my head and got back to work, only to be distracted by more yapping.

I was on my feet, realizing that the racket was coming from my backyard.

I dropped the cultivator and ran. As I got to the side of the house, a squirrel swerved in front of me and darted to my right, disappearing through the fence into Dottie's yard. A few feet behind him was a dog. Whimpering, he pressed his muzzle between the slats, with his nose twitching.

The chattering squirrel, confident he'd outwitted his opponent, sat high in a tree.

I reached to grab the dog's collar, but Jamie was faster.

"Come on, Scooter." He pulled his pet out of my reach.

"What's your dog doing in my yard?"

Before Jamie could answer, Scooter broke free and darted toward the patio.

"Oh, no!" I clamped my hand over my mouth as I watched the destruction. My beautiful flowerpots were on their sides, dirt spilling out of them. Broken purple hyacinths and yellow daffodils lay scattered on the cement.

His nose to the ground, Scooter sniffed and pawed as if he were searching for a bone.

I raced toward the dog, and this time I got him by the collar and I wasn't letting go. I found some twine under the back steps, looped it through his collar, and tied him to the railing.

I glared at Jamie. "I never ever want to see your dog again." Even as I said the words, I realized my order was impossible. Scooter had every right to be in the neighborhood—as long as it wasn't in my yard.

"You must keep him on a lead at all times." I shook my finger. Jamie nodded, his lips quivering, and I felt as if I'd ordered the shooting of a unicorn.

"How did he get here?" I asked, continuing my lecturing tone.

Jamie had zipped his lips, but his eyes gave him away. He glanced to the left and I realized he'd smuggled the dog into the yard by using the narrow cement sidewalk between the garage and Dottie's fence. The back end of the sidewalk led to the lane. All Jamie had to do was open the gate for Scooter.

I focused my attention on Jamie. "This mess must be cleaned up." I pointed to the spilled dirt and knocked-over pots. I wasn't going to let either Jamie or Scooter out of my sight until it was time to send them home. There would be no more mishaps.

Realizing that I'd sounded harsh, I tempered my next remark. "We'll do it together."

I figured this was the best way to keep the sheepdog and kid under control. Maybe I'd been too critical with Jamie, but his dumb dog certainly needed some training.

Scooter was pulling on the improvised lead and I worried he might break it. "Sit." I pointed my finger at his rear end.

He sat, and for the first time, I noticed that Scooter was a combination of dark grays on his body and hindquarters, and his paws, face, head, and chest were white. With his thick, glossy coat, he looked to be a purebred English sheepdog.

Mutt or purebred didn't matter to Jamie. He knelt, put his arm around the dog, and whispered, "It's okay, Scooter. I won't let her hurt you."

What did he think I was going to do? Kick the dog? I hated to admit how much Jamie's comment hurt. He really believed that I was a crabby old lady, the same as I'd believed about my piano teacher. My harsh judgment of her made me kind of sad now. I had never really known her, but it seemed as though Jamie had the same feeling toward me. One thing for sure, he didn't hide his dislike. I wondered how my piano teacher had felt when I stared at her, thinking nasty thoughts. Had she read my mind? I wasn't sure how or when it had happened, but I was getting more like her every day.

I couldn't change Jamie's feelings and I decided that the best plan was to get everything cleaned, put aside my annoyance over my broken flowerpots, get the dirt swept away, and take Jamie home. My part of the bargain with Mrs. Sorenson would be fulfilled and I wouldn't have anything more to do with her son.

Half an hour later, we'd achieved my goal. The patio was cleaned, and with a twinge of irritation, I remembered the food. I could picture Mrs. Sorenson's sad expression if Jamie came home with all the cookies and lemonade.

"Why don't we have the treats you brought?" I suggested.

"Okay." His answer was polite, as if he understood that "no" wasn't an option.

Jamie and I sat on the patio; he periodically dropped bits of food on the cement, purely by accident, and the sound of Scooter's chomping filled the silence between us. As I glanced at my broken flowers, which were now in a vase, I realized that Jamie and Scooter spelled disaster for my house and for me.

Chapter Four

Dottie had phoned me and suggested we go to the mistletoe party together. Good old Dottie. She can make conversation with anyone and I was glad to accompany her.

As I walked up her steps, I realized she'd been watching for me, and before I could do anything, she opened the door. Raising her arms like some high priestess, she sang out, "Ta daaa!" Her sound reminded me of trumpet fanfare from the olden days.

"What do you think of my new color?" She fluffed her hair.

Today it was flaming red, and in my opinion, it clashed with her muumuu. The shiny yellow and green material was splashed with brilliant pink flowers, all set in a jungle motif. A tropical bird could get lost in the floral pattern.

Dottie didn't fish for compliments. Before I had time to comment on her hair, she lifted her skirt a bit so I could see her shoes.

"Pretty sexy. Right?" She balanced on one foot and wiggled the other, making the beads on the toe sparkle. "I'm ready for dancing."

I figured Dottie could be ready for any sort of fun.

"Shall we go?" I held out my hand, and we walked down the stairs like two debutantes going to their first ball.

We arrived at Mrs. Sorenson's place and I could hear

people laughing. I held the screen door open, allowing Dottie to go in first. She swept by me and entered the living room. I followed.

Small groups of people were chatting and I nodded at them, before I directed my attention to Mrs. Sorenson who was sitting at the end of the room in front of the window, in the same chair she'd used when I'd come to discuss my tulips.

There weren't any flowers on the lamp table, and without them, a little bit of happiness had left the room. I promised myself that if I visited Mrs. Sorenson again, I'd bring her some flowers.

I questioned my sudden generosity. Was I really going to visit the woman and be her friend? The entire year I'd lived in my house, I'd never bothered with her. To be honest, I really doubted if I'd start now, but that didn't mean I couldn't deliver some tulips to her. I'd already missed the horticultural contest for this spring, so I'd give her what was left.

Mrs. Sorenson's living room held a curious display of Christmas decorations. A little tree stood in the corner beside the fireplace, and even had some wrapped boxes under it. Garland hung in haphazard loops over the couch and was only pinned halfway up the wall. Jamie must have stood on the sofa and taped the decorations.

I swung to my left and saw the mistletoe hanging in the archway. Across the hall was the dining room. Delicious food smells were coming from my right and I guessed the kitchen was there, at the back of the house.

It was just like a Christmas celebration, but in the spring. *I don't understand why anyone would bother with mistletoe, especially considering that it's fake.*

I overheard a woman whispering, "The poor dear soul works so hard to provide a good home for her son and she isn't well." The speaker gave a sideways glance, indicating

Mrs. Sorenson.

I scanned the room, searching for the kid, but he was nowhere in sight. I don't know if I was delighted or disappointed. Maybe I didn't want to totally seem like the crabby neighbor lady from across the street, and maybe I sort of wanted to make amends for getting so mad at his dog ... but a dog had to know his place, just like a child. Scooter shouldn't have been in my yard.

Mrs. Sorenson waved and I weaved around people, crossing the living room to greet her. I held out my hand to shake hers, but the way she raised her chin and turned her cheek toward me indicated she wanted me to give her a kiss.

I'm really not the kissing kind of person, but I leaned over and brushed my lips against her cheek.

Before I could say anything, she clutched my hand. "I'm so glad you could come."

"Thank you for inviting me, Mrs. Sorenson." When I'm at a loss for words, I resort to formality.

She held my hand. "Please, call me Elena. I want us to get to know each other better and have tea soon."

The desperation in her voice made me uncomfortable and I was glad when Dottie tapped on my shoulder and announced, in a stage whisper, that she had to talk to me. Right away.

I backed away from Mrs. Sorenson and smiled at another neighbor I recognized. Before I had any time to talk to her, Dottie grabbed me by the arm and propelled me across the room to the small foyer, where we were separated from the rest of the people. I turned my back to them.

"What's the matter, Dottie?" Her flushed skin clearly showed agitation.

"I have seen the most wonderful, handsome specimen of mankind." She fanned herself and I stifled a giggle. "He must be new in town or I'd have heard his name."

"Oh, Dottie. Who have you met now?" I tried to imagine the newest recruit. Dottie had had more dates in the past year than I'd had in five. Some of her boyfriends appeared a little suspicious—from a florid, and formerly handsome, beer-bellied playboy, whom I suspected of pursuing Dottie for her money, to an old guy with a cane and a habit for almost "falling" and groping any female in sight while he regained his balance.

She batted her eyes, the blinking of her false eyelashes making her look like some cute cartoon character—a bunny or a deer. "He's not for me, darling; he's for you!" Her voice got low and throaty. "If I was twenty years younger though? I'd be after him like a heat-seeking missile, and he wouldn't know what hit him. He's a humdinger."

With every superlative she crooned, I cringed a bit more. I wasn't interested. I hoped she wouldn't blatantly push the guy at me, making us both uncomfortable.

She pushed past me and elbowed me into step behind her, while she peered around the corner into the living room.

"I'll let you know when he appears," she whispered, as if we were on a stakeout and getting ready to nab the bad guy.

I played along, trying to be cool and convince myself it didn't make any difference if we looked kind of foolish. She could introduce me to the guy and somehow I'd figure out a way to be pleasant. I hoped he wasn't one of those needy types who lived in his mother's basement. I'd had an elderly client who'd talked me into dating her son. We'd met at a coffee shop and I had to admit, he was cute in a soft, pudgy way. However, when all he could talk about was his wonderful, understanding mother, I changed my mind.

He had explained that he hadn't realized his full potential as an artist. His wonderful mother understood his passion and agreed with him that he didn't have time for regular employment—needing to let his artistic muse develop.

I wanted to tell him to join the real world, get a job, and pay his own way.

Dottie nudged me. "Look alert, Rachel."

I took a deep, calming breath, reminding myself that meeting someone wasn't a big issue. I'd laugh, relax, and be friendly. I'd also make sure that we didn't wander under the mistletoe or else he might get ideas.

Why was I being so paranoid? No sane guy would kiss a woman on their first meeting at this kind of party. The mistletoe bothered me. Hard as I tried, I couldn't forget the high school guys wanting to catch me under the mistletoe and cop a feel while they were at it. Those days were long behind me and I wanted to get over the embarrassment and shame. So why was my heart pounding extra hard?

"Where do you think he is?" Dottie asked, facing me with a troubled expression, as though we'd let our prime suspect get away.

She returned to her surveillance and I giggled again. Anybody watching us would think we were both crazy. Dottie was fun, because she didn't give a darn what people thought.

"Oh, I think I see him."

"There he is. Take a peek. He's under the mistletoe, and he is the most gorgeous hunk of man I've ever seen."

Her exaggeration made me curious to see the guy, so I moved past her, ready to sneak a peek.

"Now's your chance. Go get him, tiger." She gave me a push and I stumbled into the living room.

Chapter Five

Before I could twist my ankle or fall, Dottie's handsome hunk caught me, supporting my back with a strong arm. He saved me from hitting the floor, but not from the shock I got when I looked up to thank him.

He'd stepped back. A smile quirked his beautiful mouth and showed off his perfect white teeth. "Rachel McGivney. It's a pleasure to see you again."

His dark, thick hair was slightly wavy, with a tinge of white at the temples, giving him a distinguished appearance. His lips were full. My cheeks warmed with embarrassment as I stared and despite my better intention, I wondered what it'd be like to be kissed by him.

When I didn't answer him promptly, he put out his hand. "You've probably forgotten me. I'm Garrett Yates."

I hadn't forgotten his name or anything else about him. In my teens, he'd been the epitome of perfection and the star of all my romantic dreams. A funny ache settled in my chest. I could never forget Garrett Yates.

"Would you care for a glass of punch?"

I nodded, my mouth suddenly dry.

I glanced around the room. Dottie had left and the kid was nowhere to be seen. Mrs. Sorenson still sat in the overstuffed chair, and people milled around chatting and laughing. I was alone in a sea of self-doubt.

I'd known Garrett Yates for twenty years. Twenty-one

to be exact. In high school, I'd fallen hard for him, developing a major crush on the high school football captain and top student. We'd been in the same honor roll photo and had worked together, for hours, on the school yearbook. I'd wanted him to notice and like me. I imagined that I'd seen interest in his eyes, but after one date he'd barely talked to me. I wasn't worth the trouble. To me, his polite indifference labeled me as trailer trash.

I don't know whether this was true, but at the time I really believed it, especially when I'd overheard the popular girls making snide comments about where I lived and where my mother worked. All the tormenting memories came tumbling back into my mind.

In no time, Garrett was back with two glasses of punch. He offered me one.

"I want to hear what you've been doing for the past few years." He put his free hand on my waist, and ushered me out of the living room and across the narrow hall into the dining room. His touch was warm and disarming. We passed under the mistletoe, but he didn't miss a step. Either he'd forgotten it or didn't want to kiss me. I tried not to be disappointed, because unlike high school, this time I *wanted* to be caught under the mistletoe, and thoroughly kissed by Garrett.

Maybe I was even hoping for a little romance in my life.

He pulled out a chair for me and then sat to my right, a couple of feet away. I could smell his aftershave. I tried not to stare at him, but couldn't help remembering the young man who inspired crushes in all the girls. The touch of gray at his temples stood out attractively against his black hair, and gave him a distinguished, sexy appearance.

"It's terrific to see you again." The keen, measuring glint in his eyes made me self-conscious.

Other guests came into the dining room. Chatting and acknowledging us with a nod, they helped themselves to appetizers from the food-laden table. I reached for some cheese and crackers, and the guests wandered out of the room, leaving me alone once more with Garrett.

As a female guest passed the doorway, she paused and caught my attention, with a knowing gleam in her eyes and an admiring glance at Garrett. I ignored it.

"I hear you're in business," Garrett said. He placed his hands on the table and I was too quick to notice that there was no wedding band. I realized lots of couples didn't feel rings were necessary. I actually agreed with them, but couldn't help wondering if this applied to Garrett.

I tried to convince myself that, if I could be calm when making renovations and design suggestions to prospective clients, I was perfectly capable of explaining my business to Garrett. I went into a few details about how I'd come back to Maryville just over a year ago, bought a house, and renovated it.

"I take it you're planning to make Maryville your permanent home?" He asked the question with great sincerity. For a few seconds I imagined that he really cared, but then wondered why he would. I dismissed the negative thought almost as quickly as it had come. My cynical feelings were getting the better of me and I knew I should behave like an adult and not some foolish, drooling schoolgirl.

"Business has been going very well," I said, warming to the interest in his dark brown eyes and feeling a blush of pleasure at being the center of his attention. He still had the ability to make my heart beat faster.

"I'm delighted for you, Rachel." He moved his hands toward mine and the flutter in my stomach climbed to my chest. Disappointment cascaded through me when he ignored my hands and picked up my glass instead. "Would you care for another drink?"

He stood and I nodded, at a loss for words. I'd

foolishly misjudged his intentions and once again I was out of step, just like a few years ago when I'd dated a guy and started to like him. He'd announced that he was looking for a wife and wanted a big family. I'd felt pressured, like I was auditioning for a part. I'd quickly dropped him. The whole scenario scared me. Maybe I was destined to live alone, like my piano teacher.

A couple moved under the mistletoe and locked their lips in a deep embrace. The woman thrust herself against the man and I looked away, embarrassed by their public intimacy. Garrett strode back into the dining room and I managed a polite nod. He glanced back at the pair and then back at me, his expression unreadable.

Jamie dodged past them and stopped beside Garrett.

"Slow down, buddy," Garrett said, putting the two glasses on the table.

"I saw them kissing." Jamie pointed to the pair who were holding hands and walking toward Mrs. Sorenson. He smacked his lips together and made sucking sounds.

Garrett ignored the display of bad manners. If the kid were mine, I'd have been on him in a nanosecond, but I chose to mind my own business. This wasn't my house and it was not my place to lecture Jamie.

My good intentions didn't last for long. Jamie yanked on Garrett's sleeve and gave him an angelic grin.

"It's your turn to kiss someone." Jamie rotated and his gaze landed on me. He tapped Garrett's arm. "You've got to kiss Miss McGivney."

I wondered how long he'd connived to get even with me.

"Come on. You have to kiss her." Jamie did a quick exit and within a few seconds, a recording of "I Saw Mommy Kissing Santa Claus" blared from the living room.

I swallowed and Garrett put his arm on my shoulder. "If you don't kiss me," he whispered, "Jamie will think of some other way to play a trick on you. Kissing me might be the least unpleasant option and it'll be all over before you even feel the pain." His eyes gleamed with amusement.

Warm excitement bubbled through me. I put on an air of confidence and said, "You're on." I stepped under the mistletoe and before I even had time to brace my feet, Garrett had pulled me into his arms.

I tilted my head back and looped my arms around his neck. I'd show that kid he couldn't get the better of me. Who was I kidding? This kiss wasn't about the kid—it was about something I wanted all those years ago and still wanted. I'd been given the perfect opportunity.

Garrett's lips brushed my mouth in a friendly gesture, as if for the benefit of those watching us. The music got louder, pulsating in my head, and something unfamiliar twisted inside me as I pictured the pair before us, ardently kissing under the mistletoe. I found myself brashly saying, "Let's really show them."

He pressed his mouth to my neck, whispering, "I've waited a long time for this." His words aroused a deep longing to experience and understand the passion I'd seen in other couples. He held me in his arms, with his thighs so close they pushed against my skirt and the warmth of his chest pressed against my breasts. I tilted my head and shut my eyes, vaguely aware of a child's laughter in the background and people cheering. Garrett's lips closed over mine. Pleasure rippled down my spine and a drifting sensation filled me, as if I'd fallen into a pillow of clouds. His kiss coiled around my senses and ribbons of sunlight danced before my eyes. I slid my hands up his back and something stirred in my stomach.

Was the world spinning or had Garrett twirled me around?

Too soon the kiss ended and the music changed to a thumping dance rhythm and people clapped in time to the beat. Garrett had one hand on my arm, and with his other hand, he'd grabbed Jamie.

Jamie held my right hand and Garrett my left as we moved into the living room. We danced in a circle, and on one of our turns, I glanced at Mrs. Sorenson.

I saw a glow around her head and shoulders and realized that I was seeing her aura. I'm sure nobody else noticed it. She wasn't smiling and yet I had the feeling that she'd discovered some treasure. A part of me wanted to understand and experience the genuine happiness radiating from her. I was almost bursting from my own ridiculously happy bubble. We lifted Jamie, swinging him until his feet flew off the floor and he giggled. People cheered and clapped.

The music stopped. My little bubble of happiness burst, and Jamie ran to his mom. She kissed him on the top of the head and glanced up at me. My heart gave a tender twist, knowing how privileged I was to witness a special moment between a mother and her son, and their special love for each other. My insides were running in a tight circle. I knew I'd never deserve a man's love or a child's trust, not after what I'd done, but I tried to ignore that knowledge.

Half an hour later, after saying our goodbyes, and Garrett telling me that he'd be in touch, Dottie and I left the party. After our kiss, I was disappointed Garrett hadn't asked me for a date. I had to remember that I'd initiated the kiss to show Jamie he couldn't embarrass me. Garrett had been a good sport. Still smitten with him, I'd allowed myself to think his kiss was for real. I doubted I'd see him again. Besides, he probably had a girlfriend.

As we strolled back to Dottie's house, she commented, "I was watching you and the handsome hunk. I think he's interested."

Chapter Six

Over the next few days, I found myself dwelling on Garrett and the kiss more than I cared to admit. His comment about being in touch hadn't led to anything. He didn't phone and although I hoped we'd bump into each other it was unlikely. I had no idea where he shopped or whether he did his own cooking, so I prepared myself to not see him again.

Maybe I'd been too forward with him. My mother had warned me about being an easy mark for some man, and I had never forgotten her advice until a few days ago—when I'd made a fool of myself at the mistletoe party. *What would she think of my behavior?*

I couldn't dwell on it, because earlier this morning, I received a surprise phone call from Mrs. Sorenson. She'd invited me for tea. I sometimes wonder why people think 'working from home' means that I don't have to keep regular hours. My business pays the bills and I have customers to please.

However, in keeping with my new policy to be more neighborly, I picked the last of the tulips and visited Mrs. Sorenson after lunch.

She opened the door. "Rachel, it's so good to see you. Please come in."

I shoved the flowers toward her. "These are for you."

Her face glowed. "Thank you so much. They're

beautiful. Jamie and you both love tulips. It's so wonderful."

It was no secret that the kid had an affinity for *my* tulips, but I wouldn't overdo any bond between us.

"Do come in. There is so much we need to discuss."

I got the distinct impression the subject would come around to Jamie. As far as I remembered, we hadn't had any arguments since the dumb dog had knocked over my flowerpots and there was the annoying incident when the dog ran in front of the car and I'd been afraid I could have injured and maybe even killed him.

Before I had time to sit down, she said, "I'll make some tea." She gave a nervous flutter with her hands and seemed to want to escape to the kitchen. "Why don't I show you our yard where Jamie plays? I hear your backyard is large like ours."

I nodded, not sure why she'd be interested in my property. I suspected she was trying to fill the awkwardness.

I followed her to the kitchen, took off my sunglasses and put them on the counter and looked outside. She was right. I guessed her yard was the standard 50 by 120 feet, with a detached garage at the rear. In the center of the lawn was a table with two lonely chairs. I wondered if Elena and Jamie sat outside for dinner.

She stood beside me and peered around the yard. "I told Jamie I'd invited you for a visit and a chat."

No wonder the kid had made himself scarce. Changing the subject, I said, "Can I help you with the tea?"

"I'm fine." She filled the kettle with water and then plugged it in. "Why don't you sit in the living room and relax?"

While I waited, I had an opportunity to look around. She didn't have much in the way of furniture. I was sitting on the same old, leather sofa, opposite Mrs. Sorenson's stuffed chair. The floor was blond hardwood, typical of many homes built in the fifties. With sanding and a new finishing coat, it could be beautiful. Despite its age and worn-down look, I still found it attractive—and reminiscent of its owner.

In no time, Mrs. Sorenson was back with a tray. She placed it on the coffee table and poured me a cup of tea. She sat in her favorite chair. I had the weirdest feeling, as though I were being scrutinized, or interviewed for a job. She kept her eyes on me and when our gazes met, she smiled and I wondered what she was thinking.

A door banged and Elena jerked forward, the noise startling her." Jamie, is that you?"

"Hi, Mom."

"Rachel's here. Come and visit with us."

There was silence and I waited for an excuse.

He didn't take long. "Scooter's outside. I promised him I'd take his photo. I'll be in later."

The door banged and Mrs. Sorenson smiled. "He's like you, Rachel, full of life and energy." She sipped her tea, placed the cup on the round table beside the chair, and then—seeming to change her mind—she picked it up again.

The pallor of her skin and the fragility of her almost skeletal frame sent a cold shiver through my body. It hurt to witness her pain and loneliness. In one way we were alike: two souls striving to find balance and happiness. She had Jamie. I had my work. When I was engrossed in it, the lonely demons disappeared and I found satisfaction. I wondered if she found the same relief in her son.

I realized she hadn't invited me just to sip tea; something more was happening—something I didn't understand. I didn't want to beat around the bush, so I asked her outright, "Is there anything I can do for you, Mrs. Sorenson?"

She blinked in surprise and cleared her throat. "I want us to know each other better. Please, call me Elena."

"Okay, Elena. Thank you for inviting me for tea, but I get the feeling ..." My voice trailed off. I raised my hands, palms up, and then let them drop to my lap, not knowing how to put the feeling into words.

She fingered the cup and finally placed it back on the table. "I've been doing a lot of soul searching." Her lips quivered, and I felt like the nastiest person in the neighborhood. Was she going to criticize me for the way I'd treated her son? I have a bit of a complex, always feeling guilty over what I could have or should have done. I guess it goes back to my childhood and what had happened—how I'd neglected my duty and it'd led to tragic results.

She stared at me. "I've always admired your energy and hard work."

There was some message in what she was saying, but I wasn't getting it. "I'm pleased you noticed," I replied, still confused.

She perked up, a faint smile giving her more color. "I have it on very good authority that you're a conscientious, hard-working woman, but I don't need to hear it from someone else. I've seen the excellent care you take of your house and garden. I imagine you've already guessed that I've struggled with medical problems for some time and that my health has declined."

"You'll get better," I said, noticing the bottle of pills she had brought with her on the tea tray, but truly believing that a woman, who I guessed to be in her late thirties, could not possibly do otherwise. It wouldn't be fair. She was too young to die, and besides ... she had a son to support.

Call me dumb or stupid or naive—I don't know which—but I'd always trusted that everything would get better. It had been my philosophy up until two days before my mom died. I had hoped she would regain her health, and that I'd have the money to take her on vacations to exotic lands, and we'd have time together—to talk and laugh and watch sunsets. All the things I had always wanted to do with her when she'd been too busy earning a living. To me, family would last forever, at least I believed other families did, even if mine didn't. I guess I didn't want to face reality.

"No, I'm not going to get better," Elena replied, rubbing her hands together and biting her lower lip. She reached for the bottle, opened it, shook three pills into her palm, and took them with water from a glass that rested, within easy reach, on the table.

She placed the glass back and smiled at me, seeming more composed.

My thoughts slipped back to the last few days before my mother died, when she lay unconscious in a hospital bed. I'd wanted to tell her how much I'd loved and appreciated all she had done for me. The nurses had assured me that I should talk to her, but I didn't really believe she understood. I didn't want to believe that Elena was dying.

I took another drink of tea to ease the rawness in my throat. I had the horrible feeling that the woman sitting opposite me was living on borrowed time.

Elena interrupted my thoughts. "I've had to consider Jamie's future."

Why did she want to discuss her son's future with me? It was too personal and intimate. I didn't want to be involved.

Undeterred by my silence, she said, "Jamie's been very quiet lately, but he knows I'm not well and I've told him that I've picked his guardian." She said the words with deliberate carefulness, as if she was afraid she'd burst into tears at any moment. I imagined she'd practiced the speech.

I stared out the window, afraid that tears would spill

down my cheeks if I blinked, and then we'd both be blubbering. From the sofa, all I could see was blue sky, and I kept thinking about how brave she was and that I'd never be so brave—not in a million years.

"I'd like you to be Jamie's guardian."

I blinked. The tears escaped and I stared at her. Had I heard her correctly?

I didn't answer. Her question made me tremble. *Why has she chosen me?*

The last time I'd seen Jamie, he'd been riding his bike with Scooter following him. The kid had stopped pedaling, and stared at me with the frank appraisal of a child. For the first time, I'd noticed his cute face, with his dark brown eyes, and brown bangs. His mother must have cut them because they were crooked.

I wondered whether he was remembering how much I disliked his dog. Had he known what his mother was going to ask me? No wonder he dodged coming inside to visit.

I leaned forward, and although my words were harsh, they were important. I wanted Elena to clearly understand me, because she might want to change her mind. "You realize I'd be very strict with Jamie?"

I wondered briefly why I had led with this thought, rather than simply refusing the honor outright, having no interest in taking on such an obligation from someone who was, no matter how fragile, a virtual stranger.

Besides, there was the subject of money. Raising a child involved lots of extra costs—haircuts, clothing, school fees and much more. I'd worked hard to stay on a budget and keep my business solvent. The extra expenses of a child could tip my finances and I never wanted to be poor again.

She nodded. "People I trust have told me that you're a fair and honest person."

I chalked the compliment up to more grocery store gossip. Of course, I always hope my clients found my prices reasonable, my work exemplary, and my word trustworthy, but they were talking about construction and interior design: walls, wiring, plumbing, paint samples, fabrics, and furniture—not my ability to take care of a child.

"I know you take food to Dottie every week and she speaks very highly of you."

I doubted the merits of having Dottie as a reference.

"Jamie is a bit of a free spirit and I'm rather set in my ways." It was my polite way of saying that he was an undisciplined little ... somehow the word "monster" seemed unfair and cruel now. I promised myself that I'd never again use that word when referring to him, regardless of how this all worked out.

"As you probably know," I continued, "I've never married and ..." I paused and chose my next words carefully, wanting to be very clear so that Elena completely understood. "I'm considered an old maid by some people. I'm very particular, both indoors and out. To be honest, I've worked really hard to get what I have and I simply don't picture myself having the patience needed to raise a child."

I shuddered at the thought of a child's dirty shoes on my silk rug. I'd bought it during a once-in-a-lifetime holiday to Turkey. The small, hand-made work of art was my treasure, and I'd spent all my savings on it.

Not deterred by my words, Elena said, "I have it on the most trustworthy authority that you'd be an excellent guardian and that with you ... my son would be well taken care of." She got up from her chair and moved gracefully, like a spirit floating toward me. She sat on the sofa and took my hand. Hers were cold and thin, and under her loose-fitting dress, she was all skin and bones. Her long blond hair had lost its shine and her pale blue eyes appeared watery. She rubbed behind her left ear and flinched.

Her pain and frailness made me uncomfortable. "What can I get you?"

She paused. "Give me a moment and I'll be fine." She took a deep breath and let her shoulders relax. She squeezed my hand and stared at me with her soul-searching eyes. I felt like a big bully who'd punched the nicest kid on the playground, but I knew it would be crueler to say yes and get her hopes up.

"I couldn't be responsible for your child, Elena. What if I allowed him to be in danger?" I gazed out the window. The sky was a brilliant blue, with no clouds in sight. I remembered another day long ago ... with a similar sky. For one particular little boy, it had ended in tragedy. Elena's face registered disbelief and skepticism, and I regretted having to be so blunt. But she didn't know who she was asking. Why had she picked me? *We aren't even friends! I hoped we could become good friends eventually ... if we had the time.* I shook my head, dismissing the thought—it was too painful. The kid was another matter, though. He and I already had a bad track record.

"You wouldn't hurt an innocent child."

"You don't know for certain." I rocked against the sofa. *How can she be so sure?* She must have been desperate for a guardian. I couldn't imagine anyone asking me for such a thing, not if they knew the truth.

I got up to leave.

The noise from the kitchen caused me to twist my head.

"Mom, can I talk to you?"

"Come in here, honey. Rachel would like to see you."

Jamie appeared under the arch, the very same location where Garrett had kissed me under the plastic mistletoe.

Scooter sat on his haunches beside Jamie, looking up at his master and then at me, as if we had some connection. It took a nanosecond for me to see my sunglasses, minus one arm, dangling from Jamie's right hand. In the other hand, he held the broken piece.

I stepped forward, taking the glasses and examining the cracked edge where the arm had snapped. "What'd you do to them?"

"Tell us what happened, honey." Elena's gentle manner only encouraged the kid to fabricate a good story.

"Scooter dropped them," he said.

His expression was one of pure innocence and I had no doubt that he conned Elena on a daily basis, however her next question pleased me as she leaned closer to her son.

"How could Scooter drop the glasses? Did he take them from the counter?" She never lost her cool and all the time she kept eye contact with Jamie. Maybe I'd been a bit fast in judging her for a patsy.

There was nothing slow about Jamie. He had a ready answer. "I saw the glasses on the counter and I asked Scooter if he'd like to wear them for a photo shoot. He said 'yes' and we went outside, but he wouldn't stay in the chair for a second picture. When he jumped, the glasses hit the table."

This time I didn't doubt his honesty, that is about the dog jumping, not the answer involving Scooter. I glared at the dog.

Elena and Jamie both looked at me, their heads cocked to the side, as if they were silently begging for mercy. What did they think I'd do? Declare open season on one sheepdog. I couldn't stand their agony so I said, "I'll get another pair."

They continued staring at me, their grim faces testimony to their disbelief.

I had to convince them so I shrugged my shoulders and let out a forced chuckle. "They're not prescription."

Elena touched my hand. "That's so kind of you. I feel your goodness."

I was glad she couldn't read my thoughts, although I suspected her son was more astute than I gave him credit for.

"Will you at least consider my request for a few days?" Elena asked, her voice quavering.

I drew a shaky breath. "I suppose. But you need to know in advance, if I *do* say yes—and that's a very big *if*—I will not take that dog."

She whispered, "I know. I'll talk to Jamie. He'll understand."

I winced at the bleakness in her eyes.

Chapter Seven

The day after Elena's big question, I was digging and leveling the dirt in the back flowerbed, all the while trying to decide if I should agree to be Jamie's guardian.

I certainly hoped Elena would live for a long time, but what if she didn't? Just yesterday, I had noticed the horrible pallor of her skin. If something happened to her, I'd be responsible for her kid. He'd be on my doorstep in a flash. *Worse still, he'd live with me! Cripes, I don't even like him!*

I smacked a lump of dirt with my spade and pulled out a weed's tangled root, throwing it into a pile. I felt guilty that I didn't seem to care enough about what Jamie was going through. Guilty or not though, I still didn't figure I'd be a suitable guardian. Surely there was someone else who could take him.

For the hundredth time, I questioned Elena's reason for picking me. In my opinion, doing regular and quality home improvements did *not* mean I was good parent material. I wondered if Dottie had been singing my praises and convinced Elena otherwise.

I wanted to march right over to Dottie's and question her, but I knew it wouldn't work. She'd come up with some logical-sounding answer. It wouldn't be totally accurate, but I'd never get the truth out of her. I knew she wanted me to get a husband, but that didn't mean she had to get me a ready-made kid as well.

She didn't know that I'd been asked to be the godparent for a young boy, ten years ago. I had refused immediately. At twenty-eight, I couldn't see myself saddled with a child, and yet here I was, ten years older, asking myself the same questions. I still received Christmas cards, along with the annual family photo, from the friend who'd asked me. All the while I had tried to convince myself that I was pleased to have remained single.

"Good afternoon, Rachel." A deep male voice sounded from behind me.

I froze as I recognized Garrett's voice. I looked over my shoulder. He strolled under the arch that separated the backyard from the front. In his dark slacks and open-neck white shirt, he looked like a magazine ad for expensive men's clothing. His jacket was slung over his shoulder; a gold watch adorned his wrist. My breath caught in my chest. Why did he have to look so handsome? His mouth twisted into a smile.

I pulled off my soiled gloves, letting them drop onto the grass, and stood up, suddenly feeling shy, awkward, and shabby in my cut-off jeans and V-neck shirt. Even my sneakers were dirty.

"Hello, Garrett." I smiled, determined to take control of the situation, as I walked toward him and extended my hand. "As you can see, I wasn't expecting company."

He took my hand, making me inhale sharply. I hoped I didn't sound like a fish that had been pulled out of the water. As he held my hand, and my gaze, a glint of humor danced in his eyes.

I pulled away.

"I realized this might not be a good time for you, but I was in the neighborhood meeting with a client and wanted to see you again."

His words made my heart leap, but I maintained my composure—hoping that Garrett's ability to make the butterflies in my stomach flutter wasn't too obvious. He'd caught me in my grubbiest clothes and I hated it. When I left Maryville twenty years ago, I vowed I would never be the girl from the wrong side of the tracks again.

"Please, have a seat." I indicated one of the patio chairs on my newly poured concrete pad. Garrett sat with the sun at his back. Opposite him, I sat with the sun pouring on my face and making me squint. Once again, I was at a disadvantage.

"After the party, I wondered if I'd see you around."

I wasn't sure whether he meant he had *wanted* to see me, or had simply noticed that he had not. I tried not to care either way. Two decades ago, I had certainly been sweet on him, but I was long past my teenage fantasies and raging hormones.

Who was I kidding? Garrett Yates still had the power to make me want more than kisses from him, but now wasn't the time to dwell on my unfulfilled fantasies. I'd come to accept celibacy as part of my life. After our passionate kiss, I doubted he'd given me any thought. His smile was encouraging, but I'd discovered that, as my business acumen increased and I'd grown more comfortable working with clients, my confidence with potential boyfriends had developed in the opposite direction. In order to protect myself, I'd erected an invisible barrier— one that protected the fragile inner me.

I shielded my eyes with my hand. "Oh, yes, the party." I tried to answer casually, as if his kiss hadn't been vying for top spot in my mind ever since.

"What do you think of Jamie," he asked, "Mrs. Sorenson's little boy?" His expression was unreadable, as if he'd asked me about the weather instead of something that had rattled my brain for the past twenty-four hours.

I blinked and swallowed. His question came out of left field. Was Mrs. Sorenson a client of his? Before parting ways the other night, I'd learned that he was a lawyer, specializing in family law.

I chose my words carefully. "I think Jamie is rambunctious and …well …" I wasn't sure what else to say. Trouble? A nuisance? More unflattering words sprang into my mind, but I kept them to myself.

"I understand that Mrs. Sorenson has asked you to be Jamie's guardian." He leaned back in the chair.

I had the unpleasant feeling that he knew more than he was saying and wasn't going to elaborate until I revealed my decision, so I started cautiously. "You're right. She has." My answer wasn't brilliant, but I still hadn't decided what I was going to do, and didn't want to get into it. He looked deep into my eyes though, and in a flash, I changed my mind, deciding I wanted to discuss it with someone. Why not Garrett?

"Her request surprised me." That was putting it mildly.

I thought I caught a flicker of emotion in his eyes. "So what have you decided?"

I raised my shoulders and then let them drop. "I don't know."

"From what I remember about you in high school, I think you would be a reliable person."

"I'm amazed you remember me." I couldn't keep the bitterness out of my voice.

"Why wouldn't I?"

I wiped my hands against my shorts, hesitating. "Well …"

He frowned.

I chose my words carefully. "You and I weren't in the same crowd. You were great in sports, captain of the football team, and couldn't be bothered with me. I wasn't worth the trouble for you to even notice. After all, I was from the wrong side of the tracks, right? Trailer trash." As much as the words hurt, I was glad I'd finally said them.

"You really know nothing about me. I was at Maryville

High School for two years. My family had just moved here when I started grade eleven."

"Oh. I thought you'd been around since..." He was there when I got to high school. By twelfth grade I had one thing on my mind, working hard at school to get scholarships and at the same time holding a part-time job to save money for university. If I admitted the truth, I was glad I never saw him during my final year of high school. He would have been too distracting.

"You were the center of attention with all the guys, and the girls."

He gave a wry smile. "Fame is fleeting. In school I only made a couple of lasting friends and I'm helping one of them out now."

He didn't elaborate on how he was helping the friend and it wasn't my place to question him.

"After high school, I moved away for university and never moved back—until recently to find that Maryville's gone from a town to city of over 70,000 people. In the last five years the population has doubled."

That's one of the reasons why I was here. I'd done my research and found that the biggest section of the population was between 25 and 49, great ages for wanting my construction, renovating and decorating services. It'd be easier to make my mark in a smaller city. There were so many questions I wanted to ask him, about his family, his job and why he moved back, but he circled around to my comment.

"I never called you trailer trash, did I?"

I wasn't sure what response I expected, but the starkness in his eyes made my heart contract. I quickly backpedaled. "Maybe not you, but your buddies did." I remembered the exact time and location.

"Tell me."

Embarrassed, I wanted to hang my head, but I wouldn't

allow myself to sound defeated. "I'd been helping my mother at the diner after school. Four of your friends came in and sat in a booth, eyeing me and laughing. After serving their hamburgers and chips, I walked away. One of them mocked me in a stage whisper and called me trailer trash."

Anger flashed in his eyes. "If I'd known, I would have punched him out."

"Maybe that would have helped you, but what you did to me was even worse. You totally ignored me." *And it really hurt.*

The muscles in his jaw tightened. "Do you know why I never laughed or joked with you?"

"Of course." I got up from the table, walked toward the back fence as if I had more important things to do than discuss the past with someone I hadn't seen in years, and then turned back, trying to look casual—as if it couldn't have mattered less. Garrett had stood up and was looking at me intently. I shrugged. "I wasn't good enough for you."

"According to your mother, you were *too* good."

"What?" In the past few minutes, I'd developed a tension headache. "You're not making any sense." Trying to ease the pain in my skull, I walked back to the patio and pulled a chair back into the shade, several feet from the table. There was no getting away from Garrett, though. He lifted his chair and placed it right beside mine, sitting down and leaning in closer. The touch of his hand on my arm washed away some of my bitter memories.

"I think we'd better sort out what really happened." His calming voice flowed over my heartache like rich cream over dry cereal.

I looked straight at him, afraid of my own emotions, and the realization of how easy it would be for me to get hurt by him all over again. Despite my best intentions, I wanted him to kiss me again.

"All right. In *your* opinion ... what happened?" I asked

my question, sounding deliberately judgmental.

Either Garrett didn't hear my tone or he chose to ignore it. I assumed it was the latter and I admired him for taking the high road, at least until he started grinning. "Your mother was quite the lady, and a real tiger when it came to you."

People had sneered at my mother before, but I'd ignored them. I'd overheard the gossip about her working all hours and leaving her poor child alone in a trailer. It hadn't hurt me. I'd been safe from the world, but it stung to have Garrett call my mom a tiger.

"By your expression, I think you've misjudged what I'm trying to say. Your mother wanted the best for you ... and that meant not having me around."

I gave him a penetrating stare. "Why? In high school you were Mr. Popular."

He laughed. "Your mother wasn't blind. She must have heard how I dated one girl after another, and she didn't want you to become just one in a string of girlfriends. She confronted me one day and told me to stay away from you."

I was shocked and self-conscious with his frank disclosure.

"Rachel," His tone was warm and caressing. "Don't be embarrassed. We're adults. We both know that flirtations and teenage infatuation can have unwanted consequences."

It wouldn't have happened to me, because ... well, I'd never been with a man. I kept a stony expression, hoping Garrett couldn't read my feelings. I'd never admitted my virgin status to anyone, because I was certain I'd be laughed at for being abnormal. In high school, Mom had always encouraged me to focus on my grades, so I'd get a scholarship to help with college expenses. Although she had strong opinions about the dangers of teen pregnancy— which she made very clear—she never actually talked about sex, making it seem taboo.

He continued, "Your mother wanted you to get a good education so that you could have options. She said that she didn't want you to be stuck in the back of nowhere. I admired her gumption and promised to tell the team to stay away from you or else I'd clobber them."

I struggled with the tightness in my chest. After my stepfather left, I remember seeing Mom crying and flipping through a pile of papers. At seven, I didn't realize that the man I adored had left us with a stack of unpaid bills. We'd been forced to sell our comfortable home and rent a mobile in a trailer park. My family life had gone to hell. Mom started working at the diner and putting in long hours. Most nights for the next ten years, I'd be in bed by the time she got home at night, and there wasn't a whole lot of communication between us. I had assumed I was at the bottom of her list of priorities, but Garrett's admission shook that theory.

I still wasn't ready to forget all my childhood doubts. They had gnawed at me for years and settled deep in my mind.

I gave Garrett a terse reply, "I don't imagine you were too concerned that I wouldn't be another one of your conquests."

Garrett raised an eyebrow, but didn't respond right away.

Loneliness settled back in. My mom had lectured me about the consequences of getting pregnant without being married. She said that the guy would take the fastest train out of town, because when the going got tough, the guy always left—just like my biological father. During her final days, as she lay in the hospital, she'd made me promise to remain a virgin till I married. And here I was, still keeping my promise and at the same time debating the wisdom of my vow—and more so since meeting Garrett again.

Garrett put his hand on top of mine. "Rachel, I liked and respected you. I saw how hard you worked and I wasn't so big of a jerk that I wanted to spoil your mother's dreams for you."

"I still felt like trailer trash."

"You weren't," he said, reassuring me as he brushed my hand.

The flutter in my middle moved up into my throat, choking me.

He moved his chair back and despite the warm day, I shivered. I sensed a change in him—from relaxed and comforting to somewhat brisk as the conversation headed down a different path.

"So can you tell me what you've decided about Jamie?" Garrett was back on track and in lawyer mode. I glanced at him. His face was taut. "Are you Mrs. Sorenson's lawyer?" I guessed that he was, but wanted it confirmed.

"Yes."

The frankness in his eyes made my hopes shrivel. I'd been a fool to think he'd come to visit me. I guess I was still the infatuated high school girl. Garrett was here to look out for Jamie's rights, and I admired him for doing his job, but I wouldn't let that persuade me one way or the other. "I think you ought to know that I haven't decided. I'm weighing the pros and cons, because I don't think I'd be the best choice for Jamie. He has a father, doesn't he?" I turned to look directly at him.

He stared down at his empty hands. "The Sorensons were divorced a few years ago. The father is not an option as a guardian."

"So what am I, the best of the remaining options?"

He focused his gaze on me. "Yes. Elena has a very short list: a colleague at work, a nurse from the cancer center, an uncle she hasn't talked to in years, and you. You're the most logical choice."

"Logical choice." The words tasted bitter. "That's hard to imagine, as she doesn't even know me, but regardless, I don't think logic is a good enough reason." I wrapped my arms across my chest.

Garrett looked away, his eyebrows gathered together in a frown. "You're not thinking clearly. Elena Sorenson sees you as a dedicated, reliable person who would be a stabilizing influence in her son's life."

My temper flared. "There's more to raising a child than being punctual and keeping him fed." I blurted out the question that haunted me. "What about love?" I shook my head, hardly even believing that we were having this conversation. "How could Elena give her child to me? She can't know if I'd ever be able to love him as if he were my own!"

"Love will come. You'll see," Garrett responded with the same confidence I remembered from high school.

I got the feeling that we were talking about two different kids, and didn't like his offhand attitude, like it was easy to simply adjust and grow to love the boy.

He gave me his most disarming smile. "I know we're asking for a huge commitment from you, but Elena is convinced you'll take good care of Jamie."

I clenched my fist, feeling that his words dismissed the importance of my career. "I have a job. Just because I work from home doesn't mean that I don't have commitments and responsibilities. I have a mortgage to pay. If you've got such a good impression of Jamie, why don't *you* adopt him?"

His eyes narrowed. He stood, and didn't say anything for a few seconds as if contemplating my suggestion. Then he paced the patio, rubbing his chin with his fist, his expression serious. "Don't think I haven't given it a great deal of consideration. Elena has brought Jamie into the office on several occasions. He's bright and lively, a regular ten-year-old boy. I find him funny and enjoyable. However," Garrett said, stopping right smack in front of me, "I'm away on business too much and Jamie would be left with a babysitter. It wouldn't work."

I couldn't keep the sarcasm out of my voice. "So what makes me the right person?"

He rubbed his forehead in a gesture that made me feel as if I were just one more obstacle in his very long day. I sensed his hesitation to answer, but eventually he did. "Do you have so little faith in yourself that you don't even realize you'd be a good mother?"

His words surprised me. I didn't want to examine my inner feelings. I was doing quite nicely without painful images being dredged up from my past. I struggled against the sudden ache in my stomach. "I'm not his mother and I don't want the responsibility." I knew my words sounded uncaring and mean-spirited, but he had to know the truth.

He appeared frustrated and disappointed. "Please reconsider." He sat beside me and rubbed his face with his hands. Then he lifted his head and said, "You'd cope and do a fine job. Jamie has lots of spunk and determination. He reminds me of you—the girl I knew in high school who worked hard to get what she wanted."

I resented him thinking he knew so much about me. What did he know about my past or my feelings? I put my elbow on the arm of the chair, and rested my fist against my chin while I eyeballed him. "Since when did you develop such divine insight?"

Chapter Eight

The metal legs of the lawn chair scraped against the cement as Garrett stood back up. "I have to get something from the car."

While he was gone, I surveyed my property. There was so much I wanted to do with the house, the yard, and the garage. Between the business and my home, my life was full and I didn't want the extra burden of a child. Jamie wasn't family. What right did Elena Sorenson—with heavy backup from Garrett—have to push me into something I didn't want?

Garrett returned and handed me a doubled-over piece of paper. "Read this."

As soon as I unfolded it, I recognized the printing. It was Jamie's. My hands shook and I wondered where all this was going.

Dear Miss McGivney,

My mom told me you might be my guardian. I promise to be a good boy and if you take me, I will find a good place for Scooter to live and I promise he won't bother you.

Sincerely,
Jamie

A lump settled in my stomach and I reread the note, taking my time to consider. I raised my head. The knot in my gut tightened. Assuming a defiant tone, I asked, "Since when have you specialized in presenting evidence for full-fledged guilt trips?"

His answer was equally harsh. "When did you become hard-nosed and skeptical?"

I stood up, glaring at him. "You don't know a thing about what I've been through, and I'd thank you to keep your little letters to yourself." I poked him on the chest and pushed the letter back at him.

He took the sheet, and before I had time to think, took my hand.

I tried to pull away, but his grasp tightened.

"Oh, Rachel, can't you give this a chance?"

His expression softened and I wondered what I'd do if he pulled me into his arms. Would I melt into them and expect violins to play?

I think not. Serenading strings only happened in movies. I wouldn't kid myself about my status with Garrett. I chose a different strategy, allowing my hand to go limp, indicating that he had no reason to hold it. He let go and I pulled away, sitting down and clasping my hands on my lap, vowing that there would be no more hand waving or raised voices. Instead of acting like the flustered female, I'd meet Garrett on terms he understood—logic and calmness. Straightening my back and looking directly at him, I said, "Give me time to think."

He raised his hand. "There is a document I want to show you before you make your final decision."

I was getting tired of the whole conversation. "Does it really have to be done today?"

"Yes."

Before I could protest, Garrett got up and disappeared around the corner.

"Psst."

An odd hissing sound, like a squeezed garden hose, startled me and I looked around the yard.

"Psst. Over here."

I glanced at the trellis that separated my yard from Dottie's. In the summer, it was covered with a flourishing Virginia creeper vine. Between the parallel slats, a hand appeared. In it was a stemmed glass filled with red wine.

I rushed over to the fence. "Dottie, what are you doing?"

"Take this," she answered in a stage whisper. "Don't you know it's customary to serve refreshments and goodies to your guest? You're not making any progress, so I'm taking up the slack."

"I would have offered him something ... later." My excuse sounded feeble and I realized that refreshments hadn't crossed my mind.

"Rachel McGivney, how are you ever going to catch a man if you let him sit there without a bite of food or something to drink? Don't you know that the way to a man's heart is through his stomach? Now take this."

I wondered if Dottie was right, so I did as instructed and took the full glass to the patio table.

"Hurry. He'll be back in no time." Another glass emerged through the fence, followed by a plate of cheese and crackers, plus red cocktail napkins.

I arranged them on the table. Garrett came around the corner and I tried to look as nonchalant as possible, while sipping my wine.

"Wow, that was fast, and a pleasant surprise too. Mind if I join you?"

"O-of course not," I stammered.

Garrett pulled out the patio chair and sat.

I figured that if I played it right, this moment could be a turning point. At least I hoped so. I knew that we didn't have a relationship or anything even remotely close to it, but I assumed Garrett hadn't taken the time to come all the way over for nothing. He could have called me from his office and talked to me. Instead, he'd chosen to visit me at home. I looked at him, expecting to meet his warm gaze. I was dreaming. His lips were drawn in a hard line, as if he were preparing to question a witness. My flight of fancy about a possible relationship nosedived into harsh reality.

I couldn't flatter myself that he'd come solely for the pleasure of my company. I realized that it only made sense for Garrett to come over after he'd seen Mrs. Sorenson. She was right across the street. It had nothing to do with me personally. From what I used to know of him, he always had a goal, and this time it was strictly business.

I waved at his briefcase, momentarily forgetting my promise to be cool and composed. "What other shockers did you bring with you this time?"

Chapter Nine

I'm not quite sure *why* I decided to become Jamie's guardian. That night, after Garrett's afternoon visit, I'd tossed and turned in bed. One minute I was for it, thinking about how much I could help Jamie. The next minute, I decided that I didn't want my perfect life disturbed. I didn't want a child underfoot. Then I flip-flopped and I was back to thinking it might be fun, and that maybe—just maybe—Jamie and I could get along.

At six o'clock in the morning, I finally decided to take the plunge. Maybe that wasn't the ideal way to describe it, but it *was* a plunge—into the unknown.

I phoned Garrett around eight, and to my surprise, got him right away. I'd planned to leave a message, but when he answered I told him my decision. The excitement in his voice was contagious and for the first time I actually believed I was doing a good thing.

"Good," he said. "The office is room 302 on the third floor. You've made the right decision. I know you and Jamie will get along."

I wasn't going to jump on the bandwagon right away and shout for joy. "We'll see," I answered, unable to keep the uncertainty out of my voice. We set up an appointment for later that morning.

In the meantime, I had work to do on redesigning a new kitchen and nook in a 1980s house. The couple who'd hired me wanted a functional, open-concept plan for themselves and their two children. I'd measured the area and suggested increasing their storage space, removing some upper cabinets, and taking out a screen divider. I had doodled and sketched in some rough ideas I'd been considering and had a pretty good idea of the cost. They had given me an idea of their budget for the project and I didn't want to go over their limit. I knew what it was like to have to make your dollars stretch.

I glanced at my watch and realized I had to leave to make it to the appointment on time.

At a few minutes before noon, I walked into the office building and took the elevator to the third floor. I tried to convince myself that I'd made the right choice. It was really too late to change my mind.

As soon as the elevator stopped and I stepped out, I saw the office number.

I opened the door and waited beside the empty reception desk. When Garrett walked down the hall, his broad shoulders filled the corridor. "Good morning, Rachel. I'm glad you could make it." He reached out and clasped my hand. My heart raced as he gazed at me, his pensive expression changing to a welcoming smile.

I swallowed, fighting to control the inner turmoil that always seemed to happen when he touched me. I had to remind myself that this meeting wasn't about Garrett and me.

He ushered me into a room with a long table and half a dozen leather chairs around it. Occupying one seat was Elena Sorenson. I was surprised to see her and wondered why she was at this meeting.

Garrett pulled out a chair for me right beside her.

"Mrs. Sorenson wanted to be here today while you signed all the paper work," he explained.

She gazed at Garrett with adoring eyes. "You've been a

pillar of strength for me. Thank you for your advice and for the kindness you've shown Jamie. He adores you."

I was getting all the work and Garrett the adoration. I immediately regretted my miserly thinking.

Garrett turned his attention to me. "Mrs. Sorenson has appointed me the executor of her will and I'll be the trustee for her estate."

I doubted there'd be much of an estate, but having Garrett take care of her financial matters probably offered her comfort.

"Mrs. Sorenson has an insurance policy that will provide for Jamie's care and his future education. I'll be overseeing the management of the money that will be placed in a trust and will be set up to provide for Jamie's expenses. You'll be sent a check each month."

I clamped my mouth shut. He'd made everything cut and dried.

Garrett nodded, indicating Mrs. Sorenson, who sat with her hands in her lap. "We've discussed the trust agreement at length and she's indicated her priorities for Jamie's care."

I wondered what was going through her mind. Why did Garrett have her attend this meeting? Wasn't this a conversation that was too hard for her to hear—the discussion of what would happen after her death?

"Thank you for explaining this to Rachel." Mrs. Sorenson gave Garrett a faint smile and then she turned to me. "I wanted you to know—Jamie won't be a financial burden on you. I believe you are the right choice and I'm glad we're together today to plan for our son."

The words, 'our son' hit me in the stomach. I'd been worried about money and not really considered the depth of her pain—giving up her son and knowing she'd never be able to attend school concerts and see him grow. I admired her courage and could only hope I'd be up to the trust she'd placed in me.

Chapter Ten

In an attempt to get to know Jamie better, I accepted another invitation from Elena and once again we sat in the living room. I sat on the sofa and Elena in her favorite chair—or so I called it.

"I told Jamie you were coming over." She glanced around, a worried look on her face. "He's probably hiding on us. Let's find him." She got up and walked down the hall to the bedrooms. I followed her. She turned to the left and said, "Jamie. Rachel's here and she wants to talk to you."

And we would talk about...? Was this the same question going through Jamie's mind? I pushed on the door to another room. It opened a little and then jammed.

"Jamie, are you in there?"

"Boo." The door flew open and Jamie jumped in front of me, his arms flapping like a scarecrow on a windy day. The dog barked and Elena came running.

She glanced from me to Jamie, her face registering shock and then she smiled. "Oh, Jamie."

He stood beside his mother and she put her hand on his shoulder and pulled him close to her side. "You might have scared Rachel and remember what I told you about making a good impression on her." Her voice was gentle as she rebuked him.

I placed my hand on my chest. My heart hammered and

I tried to take deep breaths while I glared at Jamie.

"I gave Rachel a big surprise." Jamie looked up at his mom, his face glowing like an angel. He glanced at me and frowned.

"Jamie likes to be funny." She gazed down at him. "Don't you?"

I'd replace the word funny with obnoxious.

Elena kissed the top of his head. "He keeps me on my toes and it's all in good fun."

I bit my tongue. I'd been away from kids for a long time. In my day, jumping out and scaring an adult was not considered good fun.

The rest of the summer passed and business, with the expert workmanship from Cory, was thriving. The 1980s kitchen job was complete. In the last week, I'd been contacted by potential clients who wanted to discuss a more open concept for the main floor of their two-storey house. The increased business made me happy that I'd returned to Maryville.

On a few occasions I invited Elena over for tea and although we chatted politely and she talked endlessly about Jamie, I always had the feeling that we were both waiting, like it was only the calm before the storm. Jamie rarely showed himself, and when he did, he was quiet and withdrawn.

One afternoon, as I was leaving Elena's, I heard sniffling. I checked around the side of the house and found Jamie huddled on the ground with his back against the foundation. His head was tucked to his chest and his hands covered his face. As for Scooter, I didn't see him and assumed Elena and Jamie had found him a new home.

I peered down at the small figure, wondering what to do.

He must have sensed my presence, because he slowly raised his head and brushed his arm across his red, blotchy face. He stared at me, and scowled.

Not knowing how to console him, I asked, "Can I help you?"

His face froze in a grimace, showing his intense dislike. "Go away," he muttered.

I took a deep breath, trying to compose myself after the sting of his words, and did as he asked.

That night, I lay in my bed, debating my guardianship decision. Garrett had been away on business for most of the summer. I missed talking to him, although I knew he wouldn't understand my flip-flopping regarding Jamie. Life was very black and white to Garrett, whereas I second-guessed every decision I made.

By early fall I was letting one day slip into the next without contacting Elena. I kidded myself that if she needed me, she'd call. It was easy for me to lose myself in my work and try to forget the responsibility I'd accepted.

Reality crashed in one night when I heard the crunch of tires and doors slamming. Peeking out the window, I saw an ambulance across the street. Its flashing lights cut through the darkness. I pulled on my housecoat and slippers, and ran outside. The red taillights created an eerie glow and I realized that Elena really wasn't going to cheat death. She was on a stretcher and the emergency services people were carrying her to the vehicle. Jamie, with his feet bare, was at her side, gripping her hand.

"Mommy," he whimpered. That one word ripped at my heart.

"You're taking her to Maryville General?" I asked the paramedic. "As soon as we're both dressed, I'll bring the boy to the hospital." I paused and then quietly asked the man if Jamie had time to get dressed, or if he should go with her in the vehicle now.

"You have time," answered the man.

Tears rolled down Jamie's cheeks as he stared at the back of the ambulance. It disappeared around the corner at the end of the block.

I took his hand and he didn't pull away. "Come on. We'll go inside and I'll wait while you get dressed."

He paused in the living room and stared at his mom's chair. He didn't say anything. It wasn't a time for meaningless chatter.

Two weeks later, I was sitting with Jamie and Garrett in the front row of the funeral home's private chapel. Dottie sat in the row behind us. Elena had fought a courageous battle against the malignant brain tumor that had finally taken her. I'd been with her at the hospital for her last twenty-four hours, sitting at her bedside and holding her hand, while I told her she'd been a good mother. Jamie had been on the opposite side, and now he sat tight-lipped beside me at the memorial service, with his fists balled up.

The minister's tribute was fitting and I agreed with every kind word he said. Elena had been a wonderful mother and a brave soul.

I pressed my lips together. I didn't want to cry, because if I let the tears come, there'd be no stopping them. I had to be strong for the little boy who sat rigidly beside me like a brave soldier. His lips quivered, and I wanted to put my arm around him and pull him close. I caught his eye. He turned away.

I wondered what he was thinking. Was he dreading having to come with me after the service? The kid wasn't stupid. Despite his mother's total belief in me, he understood that I hadn't wanted him. I'd tried arguing and showing her all the reasons I wouldn't be a good mother. In the end, I had succumbed to Elena's passion, Garrett's logic, and my own guilt.

All the wrong reasons for taking a child.

A small reception followed the service and a handful of people stood around, drank coffee, and offered their condolences.

Jamie remained at Garrett's side, and when he looked up at Garrett, I saw trust in his eyes. It reinforced my belief that Jamie would be far happier with his father. He needed a man for guidance and support, not a spinster—especially one who'd proved she wasn't worthy of caring for a child.

By late afternoon, Garrett had dropped Dottie off at her house and parked in front of mine. Feeling it might be easier for Jamie if we had some company, I asked Garrett in for a cup of coffee.

Garrett turned and asked Jamie if he had any cookies.

Jamie, who hadn't said a word since we'd been in the car, nodded and for the first time in weeks, I saw a tiny spark of interest. "Sure."

I handed him the house key. "Wash your hands, and then open the new bag of cookies and put them on a plate."

Jamie scampered up the steps, appearing anxious to get away from me.

Garrett put his hand on my shoulder. "It's going to be all right."

I imagined he was very good at reassuring his clients, but I wasn't easily comforted. "What have I gotten myself into? How will this ever work?" I sniffed.

He rubbed my shoulder and I wanted to collapse against him.

"Things have a way of working out. Give Jamie all your love and you'll get far more in return."

I cuffed him on the shoulder. "Since when did you

become the great philosopher?"

Warmth showed in his eyes. "Since you said 'yes' to Elena Sorenson."

I let out a deep breath and took in a slow, calming one. "I'll try to do what's right for Jamie."

He put his hands on my shoulders and I leaned forward, ready to accept a kiss. He dropped quick soft kisses on my forehead and whispered, "I have great confidence in you, and so did Elena."

Chapter Eleven

A few days later, Dottie phoned and asked if I could give her advice on sorting and donating some clothing. I told her I'd be over in a few hours, after I'd finished searching websites for furniture for my clients' condos.

I arrived at Dottie's around noon. She didn't answer after several rings, so I used the spare key she'd given me and let myself in.

Not wanting to surprise her, I called out, "Hi, Dottie! It's Rachel!"

"I'm in the basement!" Her muffled reply came from the back of the house. I followed the sound of her voice and stood at the top of the basement steps, peering into the darkness below.

"Come on down, Rachel." I looked down and saw Dottie with a bundle of clothes in her arms.

I reached the bottom, stopped, and stared. The basement was a designer's nightmare. The walls were finished with sheets of dark four-by-eight paneling. Ahead of me, and slightly to the right, was a large pool table with three round light fixtures over it that looked like they belonged in a warehouse. Their harsh glow blasted the felt, making it a sickly pea-green shade. The orange shag carpet covering the floor sent creepy chills up my spine. Left of the pool table, there was a wall that divided the games room from a media room. There were two risers leading into a dark and cramped area where I could raise my arms and put my palms on the ceiling. Big brown reclining chairs were placed in two offset rows, for easier viewing of the monster-sized television at the end of the room. More shag carpet finished off the unattractive picture.

"This was Jack's man cave." Dottie's words snapped me out of the visual nightmare and I did a 180 degree turn, facing another part of the man cave I'd failed to notice earlier—the bar. The face of it was covered with orange fake leather that was accented with three huge, orange buttons, making it look like a triple-eyed, mythological creature.

"Did you decorate this?" I asked.

Dottie beamed, and put a pile of men's clothing on the pool table. "This whole basement was Jack's baby. He was so proud of it. He'd invite the boys over to watch sports on his jumbo television, and I'd stay upstairs and prepare snacks for them."

"Jack was your husband?" She'd never mentioned his name before.

Her shoulders drooped, and she nodded. "He passed away almost two years ago. I miss him every single day."

I'd never seen Dottie be anything but upbeat. Jack must have died only a few months before I bought my house. Though I knew she was a widow, I hadn't thought about Dottie actually having a husband. I'd always thought of her as a swinging single or as someone who'd like to be one.

I tried to cover my lack of sensitivity. "I've always admired your happiness. You're always so … full of energy."

Dottie blinked. "What else can an old lady do, if she doesn't try to have a laugh? I don't have any close family, and who else would want to be with me if I complained about my aches and pains?"

"Well, you're certainly not old in spirit," I challenged,

hoping my words would cheer her.

"You've got a kind heart, Rachel. Now let's get on with the sorting." She pulled a man's shirt out of the heap of clothes and dropped it in a new pile. "I'm going to donate Jack's clothes."

"Let me help you." On my way to the pool table, I caught my foot on the step of the media room, stumbling, but managing to keep my balance. "That's dangerous," I muttered.

"Do be careful, dear," she said, indicating the risers. "I didn't want Jack raising the floor for the television area, but it was what *he* wanted, and in a marriage there has to be compromise." Her eyes took on a dreamy expression, and she looked like she would never have said "no" to her husband.

I hoped I never got so dreamy over a man that I allowed him to construct something dangerous. As a designer and decorator, I'd never allow such shoddy workmanship. My whole body itched to get rid of everything in the basement and make a fresh start. Dottie deserved a bright, cheery place, but instead of voicing my uninvited opinion, I kept quiet.

Chapter Twelve

It was the second Saturday after the funeral and I wanted Jamie to have some fun. "What would you like to do this afternoon?" I asked, as I plunged my hands into the soapy dishwater. I rubbed the dishcloth around the soup bowl, rinsed it, and placed it on the drain tray.

Jamie stood to my left. He picked up the bowl, dried it, and didn't say a word.

I scrubbed the frying pan, giving him time to decide, and hoping there was something that might capture his interest and take his mind off the loss of his mom. We'd managed the first two weeks without a confrontation of any sort and it worried me. Jamie had been very quiet and well behaved, but I couldn't ignore his pinched expression and the deep sadness in his eyes.

"Could I go ride my bike?" Jamie's unexpected question interrupted my thoughts.

I wanted him to have freedom, but I wasn't quite sure what was suitable for a ten-year-old, so I asked, "Did your mom let you ride around the neighborhood alone?"

He nodded and his dark bangs swished over his forehead, reminding me that he'd need a haircut soon. "I'm not alone. Sometimes I meet a friend."

"Oh, that's great." The thought of Jamie with a school friend lightened my heart. "What's his name?"

"Heidi."

"A girl?"

"Yes. She lives on the next block."

"Well, then, enjoy your ride." Pleased that he'd have company, I was already making plans for what I'd do when he was away. I still hadn't gotten used to having someone around while I worked. I found myself checking on him constantly, and he was probably tired of me hovering.

As an afterthought, I added, "I've been thinking about your bike actually. It's not a good idea to have it stored outside. I know it's somewhat protected under the back steps, but you and I really need to make a place for it in the garage, out of the elements."

He put his hands up, his fingers splayed, while he backed away from me. "No, no. It's okay, Rachel. My bike is fine. Really, I don't mind having it outside."

He seemed so eager to please me and not cause a problem that I decided the matter wasn't worth pursuing. At the same time, guilt washed over me for wanting time alone to work. I placed the towel on the oven door's handle, and checked the clock on the wall. "Please come home in ninety minutes."

He looked at his watch. "Okay, I'll be back by three."

"Good boy." I patted him on the head, and then quickly pulled my hand away. I sounded like I was talking to a dog. Unpleasant images of Scooter appeared in my mind. I wouldn't mention the dog, because Jamie seemed to be getting along very well without him. "You go along and play."

Before he left the kitchen, Jamie turned and said, "Thanks, Rachel."

"You're welcome." Feeling warm and pleased with his politeness, I gave myself a mental pat on the back. I worried too much. We were getting along. I rushed to finish tidying up. Jamie should have been helping me, but I couldn't forget his happiness when he'd been allowed to ride his bike. *While I have some uninterrupted time, I'd better get to my work.*

As I went to the basement office, I reflected on why I'd bought this house. I liked the lower level with its large windows, extra bathroom, and the laundry room. In addition to a huge rumpus room, I also had my own private office with a wonderful built-in bookcase and desk. The large room was the hub of my home design business.

I sat at my desk and leaned back, thinking about my latest job, knowing I should get to work. But I was too busy feeling satisfied over how well I was coping with Jamie. I glanced around the room. My gaze stopped at a package that I'd left on the floor. It was about the size of two shoe boxes put together. I picked it up and felt my heart skip a beat. Elena had given it to me before her death, telling me that it contained mementos Jamie would cherish one day. I didn't think that so soon after his mother's death was the best time for him to see it. Perhaps later we would look at it together. If I checked it out though, I might get a better understanding of Jamie's family, and especially his dad.

I lifted the cover. On top were a few Christmas cards from last June, sent by friends who had obviously bought into Elena's "Under the Mistletoe Party" idea.

I remembered feeling critical, and questioning why anyone would have a mistletoe party in the spring. I'd discovered the answer only too soon. What had she thought when I hadn't taken her a gift, or even a card? Under that top layer of Christmas cards, I found Jamie's birthday cards. One had a friendly-looking octopus lounging in a bath, with eight legs dangling over the tub's edge and bubbles floating in the air. Inside was a verse and some handwriting:

Dear Jamie,
Lots of love on your tenth birthday,
Dottie.

I hadn't even given his birthday any consideration, let alone sent a card.

The thickness in my chest increased as I viewed photos of Jamie and Elena. I hoped to find some baby photos, but there were none ... and to my disappointment, there were no pictures of the whole family together.

I flipped through more photos, ones showing Jamie dressed in ski pants and a parka, playing in the snow and climbing drifts. Another photo showed Jamie and a man I took to be his father, each holding a fishing rod and the fish they had caught. Once again, Jamie's eyes weren't on the camera. He was too busy grinning at Walter. All my positive views about how well I was doing as Jamie's guardian vanished. I wasn't the right person. Jamie had never once looked at me with love in his eyes. Why would he? I hadn't shown *him* any love.

In the past few weeks, I'd been the dutiful caretaker, feeding Jamie, making sure he had clean clothing, and getting him to bed on time—the same treatment you'd give a pet, but not a child who needed extra love.

Why hadn't Elena wanted Walter Sorenson to take Jamie? I'd questioned Garrett about the ex-husband and he'd tersely replied that Elena had emphatically stated she didn't want any connection with him. What did Walter think? Wouldn't any father want to know? What about Jamie? As far as I knew, nobody had asked his opinion. I'd always wanted to be with my stepfather, but never had the chance. Why would I take that choice away from Jamie? Shouldn't he have the right to decide?

There was only one way to find out.

I took out a piece of paper and penned a short note to

Mr. Sorenson. I could have typed it on the computer, but somehow I hoped the father might respond better to a hand-written note.

I finished the letter and tucked it into an envelope. I'd look up the address, but I wouldn't send it until I found the right time to discuss the subject with Jamie.

Chapter Thirteen

The front doorbell rang. I shoved the envelope between two books on an upper shelf, where Jamie couldn't possibly see it, and then I scampered up the stairs, yelling, "I'm coming!" I hoped whoever was there hadn't decided to leave.

Dottie stood with a plate of tarts in her hand.

"Come on in."

She walked into the living room, and glanced around as if she was looking for someone. "I haven't seen that handsome man around here lately."

"I've been much too busy," I lied, trying to discourage Dottie from probing any further.

She flicked me on the shoulder. "As soon as you stop thinking about men, Rachel McGivney, you'll know you're dead." She swiveled to the left and grinned. "You're not hiding him, are you?" Her eyes twinkled and she tilted her head, indicating the direction of my bedroom. I made a face, pretending her insinuation had scandalized me.

Dottie seemed to be back in her usual form. If she hadn't confessed about her husband, Jack, I never would have guessed that she missed the love of her life. She put on a good act.

Without waiting for an answer, she rushed on, "I can't see your bedroom window from my front room, but if I take a walk past your house and see that the curtains are closed and the hunk's car is outside, I'll know you're making progress." She winked. "Know what I mean?"

"It isn't going to happen, Dottie." I wasn't being quite honest. I *had* considered Garrett Yates ... and the bedroom.

"Aren't you going to invite me to sit?"

Before I had time to reply, she sashayed toward the couch.

I raised my hand. "Please don't walk on my rug." It was in front of, not under, my coffee table on my gleaming hardwood floor. I wanted the rug on display without furniture indentations.

Dottie stared at the rug and then turned to me, her forehead a mass of wrinkles. "Why not? Rugs are on floors to be walked on."

"This is the special silk rug I bought in Turkey," I said, admiring the intricate pattern. "It's hand-woven."

"Well, la-*di*-da." Dottie raised her hands in the air, rolled her eyes, and strolled toward the sofa with an exaggerated swing to her hips. She didn't step on my rug— my beautiful, little, three-foot-by-five-foot work of craftsmanship.

"What you need to do with that," Dottie said, pointing to my rug, "is frame it and hang it on the wall." She let out a big sigh as she placed her plate of tarts on the coffee table. "When are you ever going to understand what's really important in life?"

Dottie had taken one of her conversational quantum leaps.

"I'm not following you," I replied.

"I'll make myself perfectly clear." She put her fists on her hips. "When are you going to hook up with the hunk?"

"He has a name, you know."

She gave me a seductive wink. "Who cares? All the gods on Mount Olympus would kill for his body."

I steered the conversation back to reality. "There's no reason why I'd be in contact with Mr. Yates." I'd received the first payment from Jamie's trust account. Garrett had signed the check, but hadn't included a note or any correspondence directly to me. I'd never admit to Dottie that the relationship I had with Garrett was strictly business, at least it appeared that way to me. I'd hoped it might blossom into something more.

"If he's too slow to get into action, why don't you just phone the guy?"

"It's not my place to phone him. Besides, I'm sure he's too busy with clients."

Dottie let her hands drop to her side and groaned. "For a pretty girl, you sure are a slow learner. Phone him and give him something else to consider."

"It wouldn't be proper," I protested. "Besides, I don't believe in chasing after a man."

"Why not? When you see the target," Dottie said, drawing an imaginary circle in the air, "you go after him and then ... bang!" She stabbed the bull's eye. "You've got him. Phone him, text him, email him ... whatever all you young people do."

Before I had a chance to protest, she continued. "With your antiquated ways, you'll never catch a man. If you can't think of anything else to talk to him about, there's always the kid. Use him as bait."

I choked at her suggestion. "And how is that supposed to work?"

Dottie shrugged. "I don't know. You're the designer. Get creative."

The heat was rising up my neck. I liked Garrett, but what if he didn't return the feeling. Was he only being polite? In the early days of my career, I'd worked for a small company. I'd fallen for my boss. He was gentle, handsome, and always complimented my work. I'd gotten the wrong idea, thinking that liking my work was the same thing as liking me.

At the Christmas party that year, I had too many drinks and made a play for him. It wasn't appreciated, and a few weeks later—when a decision was made to downsize the company—I'd been let go. After that episode, I'd made two promises to myself. From then on, I'd only drink in moderation and I'd never again chase a man. Garrett wasn't going to be the exception.

Determined to control the conversation, I changed the subject. "Jamie will be home soon and I want to prepare supper. I have to get the potatoes boiled and the chicken baked."

Our conversation stopped. I heard talking outside. Glad not to have any more prying comments, I took the opportunity to answer the door. I was surprised to see Jamie standing there, with Garrett behind him on the step. They were grinning as if they were both in on some scheme.

Garrett gave the explanation. "I was driving home from work and saw Jamie biking around, so I offered him a ride and I put his bike in the trunk " Our eyes met and I believed I saw a spark of interest. "I'll be on my way." He stepped back, preparing to leave, although I thought he looked somewhat hesitant.

A tiny voice in the back of my mind urged me to say something. Anything.

I didn't have to.

Dottie elbowed past me and latched on to Garrett's arm, waving her finger. "You're not getting away without having dinner. Rachel is cooking chicken for the three of us and she's going to peel potatoes. You, Jamie, and I are going to have a nice talk, while Rachel gets the food ready."

She pulled ahead of Garrett so that he couldn't see her face, and started mouthing words at me: *"Go on, and get supper ready."* She nudged me, like a dog herding sheep.

I obeyed. Relieved not to have to make small talk, I headed for the kitchen.

I'm not much of a cook. Living alone, I've eaten a lot of raw fruits and vegetables. In the past, after a late appointment, I'd often just pick up a sandwich from the neighborhood deli.

If anyone was relying on my cooking, they'd be disappointed. I have a limited number of recipes. Of course, that particular shortcoming didn't preclude me from reading a cookbook, and expanding my repertoire, but tonight I thought I'd stick with chicken and mashed potatoes. It wasn't inspired cooking, but Jamie liked it. It was his comfort food.

I washed the tomatoes, lettuce, and other vegetables, getting them ready for the salad.

From the living room, I heard Dottie's animated voice and envied her ease with people.

"Can I help set the table?" Jamie's question startled me. He stood at the entrance to the kitchen, as if he needed permission to enter. I suspected he was as uncomfortable as I was.

"Great, Jamie. We'll eat in the nook. You can use the same place mats we always use."

His offer pleased me. Maybe I wasn't such a bad guardian after all.

After we'd finished eating, Dottie made a not-so-subtle comment to Garrett. "Why don't you help Rachel with the dishes while Jamie and I check on his homework?" She was out of her chair and ushering Jamie out of the room before I had time to say anything. I started to clear the table.

Garrett said, "Being as I've been given instructions to help, I'd better not disappoint Dottie."

I had my hands full with plates and cutlery. "It's okay," I said over my shoulder, "you don't have to stay if you've got more important things to do." I walked around the corner into the u-shaped kitchen. I was deliberately pushing him away because I didn't want him staying out of any sense of obligation. I started rinsing dishes and stacking them.

Garrett stood beside me, his shoulder inches from mine, as he placed glasses in the left-hand sink. "You won't get rid of me that fast," he replied with a wink. "It's nice to have a day off. I've been so busy travelling to Calgary and recently an unforeseen case came up in Edmonton."

I waited for him to give me a hint, but at the same time, I realized he'd be breaking lawyer-client relationship. However, it helped to explain some of his long absences during the summer.

The spicy smell of his aftershave lingered in the air. I tried to ignore his closeness and continued rinsing.

"So, what do you do in your free time?" I asked, making the question sound casual.

His eyes twinkled. "Are you asking me if I have a girlfriend?"

I shifted my weight and tried to laugh off his question while I scrubbed a pot. "Well, I *have* wondered if you had someone."

"No." He shot me an amused look. "And you? Hasn't the lovely Rachel McGivney stolen any man's heart?"

I knew he was joking, but my breath bottled up in my chest. I shook my head and stared at the faucet, my mouth too dry to talk.

"Interesting," he said quietly. I wasn't sure if I'd heard him correctly. I picked up some cups to put in the dishwasher, and without thinking, spun toward it. My breast brushed against his arm.

I caught his look of surprise and pleasure, but

pretended not to notice as I opened the dishwasher and leaned over.

Out of the corner of my eye, I saw him watching me, standing unnaturally still. Just to fill the silence, I said, "You know, Dottie means well. I'm sorry if she embarrasses you." I closed the dishwasher.

He leaned against the counter, collected and composed. "I think she embarrasses you more than she does me."

There was nothing else for me to say but the truth. "She does."

"Do you want me to stay or leave?" He spoke in a calm and deliberate manner.

"There's no rush." I wasn't about to admit that I wanted him to stay. Wanting spoke of something else that unsettled me.

He looked down at me. "Rachel, do you want me to stay?" he asked again.

I wasn't about to repeat the word. It spoke of yearning. "Of course I'd like you to stay." I closed the dishwasher, avoiding his gaze. A fluttery feeling filled my stomach.

"Good. Let's get the kitchen cleaned." He picked up a damp cloth. As he wiped the table and straightened the chairs, he said, "You've done a nice job of remodeling. This kitchen is very bright and cheerful."

A warm glow of satisfaction simmered in me. "Thanks. I've worked hard on it. I've always wanted a place of my own."

I cleaned the counter, feeling more comfortable with casual conversation about the house. "I bought the table and chairs at a garage sale—stripped the paint, ripped off the fabric—then refinished the wood and reupholstered the chairs. It sounds easy, but it's taken a lot of hard work. I've been really pleased with my success though, and thrilled with the material." I stopped chattering, glanced at the red, patterned fabric on the chair cushions, and then at Garrett.

Open admiration showed in his eyes. "It's very nice. I've noticed Jamie seems to have settled in here quite well."

His quick subject change made me realize that our primary connection was Jamie, and although he hinted at more, I knew I shouldn't allow myself to imagine anything else.

"So far Jamie has been the perfect child. But that's exactly what scares me," I confided. "I've never seen such good behavior from him."

Garrett laughed. "Boys will be boys. I'm sure he'll be up to some mischief before long."

We didn't have time for more discussion, because Dottie entered the kitchen with Jamie right behind her.

"I'm pleased to hear you young people getting along so well." She made it sound as if we were two teens who'd met for the first time at a country picnic. Dottie motioned to Jamie. "This young man's ready to go to bed and I'm going home. Garrett, why don't you see me to the door?"

I assumed she had something private to discuss with him, so everyone said goodnight in the kitchen, and Jamie and I went to his bedroom.

I'd finished tucking him into bed, and was heading toward the living room, when I heard Dottie's voice. I stopped and listened.

"Do you like Rachel?" Dottie's blunt question made me flinch, as I waited for Garrett's answer.

"She has many fine qualities." His deep rich voice made my heart flutter.

"Quit your lawyer talk," Dottie scolded. "Do you *like* her?"

I winced at her emphasis on the word "like" and her entire approach.

"Of course I like her. I've always admired Rachel."

His answer was mannerly and I wondered what else Dottie had expected him to say.

"If you like and admire her so much, why don't you get off the pot and ask her for a date? Both of you are getting older, and I know she'd say yes."

I gritted my teeth and put my hand on a door casing, allowing myself time to take a deep breath, wishing Dottie wasn't so pushy.

"I might." There was hesitation in his voice, and I hated having Dottie pester him. No guy wanted to be forced to go on a date.

But Dottie was like a dog with a bone; she didn't give up easily. "It's time for you to stop dragging your feet. I want to see some action." She stomped her foot and I could picture her shaking her finger under his nose. "I'll get out of here now, and you'd better ask Rachel for a date before you leave. Don't let her give you any guff about having to stay home with Jamie. At the drop of a hat, I can be over here and babysit my little darling, so don't take no for an answer. I've got a key for her place and she's got one for mine. I can easily come and go."

"I guess I can't do anything else." He sounded amused.

"Now you've got the idea. I'll get out of here so you can get to work."

The door banged.

Steeling myself to confront Garrett, I rounded the corner into the living room and eyed him. Before I lost my courage, I plunged right into the issue. "I overheard Dottie forcing you to ask me for a date. You don't have to do that just because she can't stop herself from badgering you."

"We're not talking about Dottie. You're my priority." His voice was liquid-smooth, suggesting something more.

I wanted to believe that I was his priority because he desired me. But was it really because of Jamie?

I was standing a few feet away from him when I saw him glance at my mouth. His eyes narrowed suddenly, as if they were fixated on my lips while a soft smile played on his own. He stepped closer, putting his hands on my arms as though to reassure me. The smell of his aftershave coiled around me and I wondered if he'd kiss me.

Instead, he took my chin in his hand, his gaze so intent, it made me anxious. "Let's get something straight, right now. Nobody forces me to do anything I don't want to do, so if I ask you for a date, it will be my choice. Dottie's badgering, as you call it, will not influence my actions. Now, have I made that point clear?"

The directness of his question made me step back. "Yes. Very." I pressed my lips together, and bowed my head so that he wouldn't see my disappointment or the fact that—once again—I felt like a seventeen-year-old from the wrong side of the tracks, infatuated with a guy who wasn't interested in me.

Chapter Fourteen

For the next few days I worked on my client's new open concept main floor design while Cory got estimates on the electrical and plumbing. With Jamie at school, I had time for long stretches of uninterrupted work. Even after Dottie's prodding, Garrett hadn't asked me for a date. As much as I tried to consider him just an old acquaintance, I couldn't stop thinking about him. Annoyed with my wimpy behavior, I thumped my fist on the desk. What was wrong with me? I was getting more referral jobs—a very positive indication that people were pleased with my work—so why wasn't I satisfied with my life?

Maybe not hearing from Garrett had reminded me of another embarrassing incident from my past, when a popular girl, named Devyn, invited me to a post-football-game party We'd known each other since elementary school. Although she was one year younger than me, it hadn't stopped us from becoming best friends. Much to my disappointment, our friendship changed after I entered high school. We'd gone our separate ways until the next year when she'd entered high school. Between classes we'd waved at each other in the hall and I was thrilled to receive an invitation, from her, to a party. After the football game, as we were crossing the field to get to her car, a guy called out.

"Before we start partying, why don't you drop her?"

I heard his words clearly and understood exactly what he meant. However, Devyn turned to him and said, "Sorry, did I drop something?"

I wasn't sure if she'd heard him correctly or pretended not to. The guy didn't say anything more, but for me, his spiteful comment took all the fun out of the evening. I left early, making the excuse that my mom had told me to be home early.

That old hurt was still there, along with a new realization. Maybe I'd been dropped by Garrett.

Determined to stop feeling sorry for myself, I decided it was a good time for a break. With all the meals I'd been preparing for Jamie, I needed to get a few groceries at the store. I'd be able to make a quick trip and be back before Jamie got home.

At the supermarket, it didn't take long to pick up what I needed. In the parking lot, I was pushing my cart to the car when I heard a familiar voice.

"Hi, Rachel. How have you been doing?" Garrett walked toward me.

I'm a pushover for guys in dark suits, with white shirts and ties. They always remind me of James Bond, and Garrett had the build to fit any action star I could imagine. I hoped my puppy adoration wasn't too obvious. "I'm very well. And you?"

He grinned. "I've been thinking about Dottie's comment."

Feeling self-conscious, I asked, "What words of wisdom has Dottie been spieling now?"

He seemed to find my discomfort entertaining, because I thought I saw a sparkle in his eyes. "Would you like to go to a movie this weekend?"

I gulped. I was really out of practice on the whole dating scene. "Uh ..."

Garrett continued, "We could see an action movie."

When I didn't answer, he said, "Or something less violent maybe. How about *Love Forever*?"

I'd seen the trailers for that one, and was certain that I didn't want to be sitting beside Garrett as the couple on the screen pawed at each other and crawled in and out of bed, sans pajamas.

I cleared my throat. "An action m-movie would be fine." Apparently, I'd suddenly developed an interest in car chases and gunfire.

Garrett smiled. "I'll pick you up Friday at six."

"Sounds good to me," I replied as I popped the lid on the trunk. Garrett helped me lift the groceries into my car and I feigned calmness while my hands shook.

On Friday evening, Garrett proved to be an attentive and gracious date, making me feel like a princess.

After the movie, we sat in his car in front of my house. An awkward silence followed. I wasn't sure if the happy couple was supposed to kiss or not. I was ready to leap out of the car, when I glanced up and saw Dottie standing on the sidewalk.

In a flash, Garrett was out of the car and questioning her. "Is something wrong with Jamie?"

"Everything's fine." Dottie beamed, looking like a little painted doll with her rouged cheeks and red curly hair. She handed Garrett her set of keys, and in her sweetest voice, said, "Why don't you unlock the door?"

I started to follow Garrett up the walk, but Dottie pulled me back and whispered, "I saw you clinging to the passenger door. You aren't making *any* progress with the dreamboat. Now get him in there and work your magic."

"I'm not sure this is such a good idea," I objected. The last time Dottie had embarrassed me. Why would tonight be any different?

She nudged me. "Don't be silly, girl. Opportunity strikes. Don't fumble the ball this time."

Once we were inside, Dottie grabbed her coat from the entrance closet. "Jamie is sound asleep. We had lots of fun and now it's your turn." She addressed the comment to Garrett, and then turned to me, and gave a knowing wink.

My cheeks burned and I gripped my fists.

"Thanks again, Dottie," I said, as she held the stair rail with one hand and waved with the other.

Garrett was behind me, and waved to her. "She's quite the lady," he said.

I caught the screen door, so it wouldn't slam shut and possibly wake Jamie. I leaned against the casing and nodded. "Dottie shoots from the lip." I pretended to laugh and succeeded in making a phony huh, huh sound.

"Actually, I find her quite refreshing." His gaze held mine, making my heart contract.

I forced my emotions to disconnect. "Would you care for a cup of coffee?"

"Sounds good." He looked into my eyes and raised an eyebrow, apparently waiting for me to make the next move.

My stomach fluttered and I glanced away, heading into the kitchen. Without another word, he followed, while I tried not to notice his closeness.

While he sat at the table, I made the coffee and put cookies on a plate.

"How do you like your coffee?" I asked.

"Anyway you make it is fine with me."

His words were a bit too personal and I glanced at him, too shy to hold his gaze and acknowledge that I understood his real meaning. I wondered what was going on in his mind. In high school, I'd remembered admiring his dark brown eyes, but I'd never realized how striking they were, sparkling with flecks of gold. The clamor in my chest made it hard for me to think, and I didn't want to do anything clumsy or say something stupid. I realized I wanted to make a good impression on him.

No. I didn't want to make a good impression; I wanted to wow him, to have him as attracted to me as I was to him. The counter that separated us felt as wide as a river and I didn't know how to bridge it.

After we'd finished our coffee, I stood at the end of the counter, my right hand on the raised section.

Garrett got up and stood in front of me. His hand slid over mine and he stepped closer. My heart pounded. I had a weird, tight feeling in my chest. As he put his arms around me, my pulse leaped into overdrive. He caressed the nape of my neck and I couldn't stifle the soft moan that escaped my lips.

"Do you realize how long I've waited to do this?" he whispered close to my ear, inhaling my perfume with his next deep breath.

I pictured how this night could progress and my nervousness forced me to say, "You might be disappointed with me."

"Let me worry about that." His lips brushed my cheek, triggering a tidal wave of longing that crashed through my body. I moved closer to him, yearning for more.

But it wasn't to be. In that moment, a little voice asked, "What are you guys doing?"

I pushed away from Garrett and whirled around. Jamie stood at the entrance to the kitchen, rubbing his eyes.

"Is something wrong?" I moved closer to Jamie, examining him—looking for a problem.

His eyes opened wider and he stared at Garrett and me with a mischievous grin. He pointed both hands at us. In a sing-song tone, he chanted, "You two were kissing."

"No!" I took a breath and let it out slowly, continuing

in a more measured tone. "I mean no ... we weren't."

He doubled over at the waist and giggled. "I saw you." He smacked his lips together and made sucking sounds. "I saw you. You were *doing it.*"

Heat crawled up my neck and my face burned. Beside me, Garrett coughed. Out of the corner of my eye, I saw him shake his head and grin.

"That is enough, Jamie." I took him by the arm and marched him out of the kitchen. "Why are you out of bed? You should be asleep."

"I needed to go to the bathroom."

"Then do it." I followed Jamie down the hall while he giggled, hugged himself, and mimicked kissing.

"You're not funny. Get going." I nudged him into the bathroom and he closed the door. I crossed my arms over my chest and leaned against the wall, my heart thumping.

Garrett paused at the end of hall. "This isn't a good time for me to stay. I'll leave." He was gone before I even had time to say goodbye.

What should I have said? Maybe I should have laughed. Some people could turn anything into a joke. Not me. I heard Garrett chuckling as he left, though.

The toilet flushed, and I turned my attention to Jamie, calling to him through the door. "Make sure you wash your hands, and use plenty of soap."

Jamie was out of the bathroom and into his bed without a word, his face expressionless, and I went back to the kitchen. The phone rang and I checked the call display. It was Dottie. What did she want at this time of the night? I picked up the receiver. "Yes, Dottie?"

"I saw Garrett get in his car, and drive away like a bat out of you know where. What did you do to scare him off?"

I wanted to scream that the kid had interfered and the man of my dreams had walked out, but I held onto my temper and lied. "Garrett only stayed for a quick cup of coffee."

"Did you take special ops training in how to discourage a man?"

I'd had enough of her comments. "Oh, Dottie, leave me alone."

Early the next morning, I sat at my desk in the basement, checking my emails and trying to laugh over what had happened the previous night, as well as at Dottie's question about special ops training. Maybe she was right. Maybe I did have a talent for discouraging men.

Before meeting Garrett, I'd come to accept my celibacy as my permanent way of life and it hadn't bothered me, or so I liked to convince myself. Garrett's appearance had upset the status quo. I should have laughed when Jamie caught us kissing. Then Garrett might not have bolted for the nearest exit. Due to my anxiety, I'd resorted to anger.

Thinking about Garrett wasn't going to get my work done so I opened my email and saw a message from a potential client. The word "urgent" popped out at me. It was from a woman who'd contacted me via email a few days earlier. She'd mentioned that I'd done her friend's kitchen and she'd liked it.

The email indicated that her husband had just arrived home from a business trip and they both had time to see me *this morning* ... if I could make it.

I didn't want to lose the business, so I emailed back, assuring her that I'd be over within the hour. I planned on offering tips on where we might start the project. I'd have to get a sense of how much money the couple wanted to spend, their time frame, and what they wanted to change in each room.

I heard footsteps above me and hustled upstairs.

"Good morning, Jamie."

As I entered the kitchen, he looked up and nodded. The wicked gleam I'd seen in his eyes last night had been replaced by a somber expression. He was seated at the table, and had remembered to put a place mat under his bowl.

I mentally patted myself on the back. Jamie was learning some good table manners. I didn't mean to be critical of his mother, but she had let him run wild. I considered manners to be part of his training, and I was pleased with my results.

I decided that I'd put the embarrassing incident with Garrett behind me and get on with my life, as if nothing had happened. Focusing my attention on Jamie, I said, "I've had a call from prospective clients and they'd like to see me this morning. I'll phone Dottie and ask her to come over."

Jamie fiddled with his cereal.

I'd made the tragic mistake of leaving a child on his own before and I was concerned about leaving Jamie. At the same time, I wanted him to understand why I couldn't afford to lose a client. When he didn't say anything, I tried to explain. "You do realize this is my job. I don't go to an office and I don't have regular hours. If a client wants to see me, I have to be available."

I gave him the long spiel, hoping he'd understand. I phoned Dottie but all I got was a recording, so I left a message.

"I'm okay by myself, Rachel." Jamie insisted.

I shook my head. It didn't feel right leaving a ten-year-old at home alone. I'd never checked the law and didn't know if there was a minimum age when kids could legally stay by themselves. I'd been left alone plenty, but that was a different time, when Maryville was much smaller. "I'm not sure about leaving you without an adult."

"I'll stay inside. I won't ride my bike." His sincerity

melted my heart and I had an inspiration. "Would you like to come with me?"

He looked horrified. "I promise I'll be here. I don't mind being alone."

It dawned on me. Maybe Jamie wanted a break from this over-anxious adult. "What will you do?"

The question caught him unawares. He shrugged. "I don't know. I'll play on the computer. Watch TV."

"Oh, Jamie. You know I don't believe in spending all Saturday morning in front of the television. I'll give Dottie another call." I punched the numbers, but nobody answered. I hung up, and then tried again.

No luck.

Jamie sat at the table, biting his lips. "I'll read a book."

He seemed so eager to assure me that he'd behave, but I wasn't totally convinced. I couldn't afford to lose a job though, so I offered encouraging words, "I'll get back as quickly as I can. There's milk and plenty of fresh fruit if you get hungry. If you hear the bell ring, look out the window, see who it is, and don't open the door unless it's Dottie or Garrett. Do you understand?"

For a few seconds after receiving so many directions, he looked a little stunned, but quickly regained his composure and answered. "I'll do everything you said. I'll be okay by myself." The honesty in his expression made me trust him.

Chapter Fifteen

By early afternoon, I'd finished discussing renovation and remodeling ideas with my new clients. I had reviewed everything with them, from what walls would be knocked down and how we'd reconfigure the kitchen.

When I arrived home, I parked the car on the street, grateful that the weather had stayed nice and we hadn't had an early October snowfall. I did a little jig on my way up the sidewalk.

I glanced up, hoping to see Jamie at the window. Would he really be interested if I told him how pleased the homeowners were with my decorating ideas, and how being a general contractor was another step in establishing my business?

Probably not.

He was a child. Floor plans, knocking down walls and paint colors wouldn't be of any interest to him. I'd tell Dottie. She always encouraged me. I wondered whether she was home.

I got out my keys and opened the door. I moved into the foyer and sniffed, surprised by an unpleasant smell that lingered in the air. Glancing into the living room, I saw Jamie tugging on a leash that was attached to Scooter's collar. "Come on, boy," he urged.

My mouth dropped open, words deserting me.

Jamie pulled and pulled, but Scooter wouldn't budge.

He was busy doing his business.

On my silk rug.

Brown poop curled and plopped down onto it and I shuddered, silent for a moment before recovering my senses. "Stop that dog!"

I wasn't fast enough. Another brown spiral squeezed out. Scooter gazed up, giving me a satisfied, stupid look and one final grunt. Then he scratched my rug with his hind feet.

I charged toward him and yanked on his collar, but the surprised bark at my action didn't help. The damage had been done. My beautiful carpet was ruined.

My question was so forceful that it came out as a clipped statement, one single, shaking word at a time. "What—is—he—doing—in—here?" I pointed to the mutt, who was now sitting next to Jamie.

"I'm sorry, Rachel; I really am. I wanted to play with him." In Jamie's big, brown eyes, I saw his plea for forgiveness.

"Where'd he come from?" I turned about crazily, as if I'd see some evidence as to where he'd been living for the past few months.

"The garage."

His answer was so simple, it confused me. "What do you mean?"

"I keep Scooter in the garage." He repeated it slowly, as if I were stupid.

I scowled at Scooter. I swear he was smiling back at me, pleased with his revenge. "You were supposed to find a place for him." I focused on Jamie, with my arms crossed over my chest, my fingers tapping, and my face contorted into a scowl.

"Don't you remember that I told your mother I wouldn't take the dog?" I didn't give Jamie time to answer. I stabbed my finger at Scooter. "Get him out of here and come back immediately." I put my hands on my hips and grimaced. "You've got a lot of explaining to do, young man."

In no time, Jamie was out of the house and I was using paper towels to scoop the poop from the rug. I cleaned as much as I could, and then went to work on it with chemicals.

I was down on my hands and knees, scrubbing furiously, when I heard a bang and Jamie stomped back into the living room. He sat on the floor, several feet from me, with his lips pressed together and his eyes red.

Tension was thick in the air and I yelled, "Explain, young man!"

Jamie's expression was defiant. "Scooter is my dog and I love him."

"You can't keep him! Look what he's done to my rug!" The creamy white fibers near the edge were now a repugnant shade of brown. "I can't get the filthy stain out." I stabbed at the spot.

Jamie scrunched his face and glared at me. "I hate your rug."

I shook my finger. "I didn't work for hours to buy art that I love, just to have it pooped on by a dumb dog."

Jamie put his hands on his hips. "He's not dumb; he's not! He's a good dog!"

We could argue day and night and nothing would change for either of us. Once again, I questioned Elena Sorenson's choice of a guardian, and questioned my sanity for agreeing. "Your dog must be gone as soon as possible. Do you understand me?"

Jamie lowered his head. I shouldn't have yelled at him, but he couldn't possibly comprehend how much I'd loved the carpet and what it meant to me.

He raised his head. His lips were set in a defiant curl. "I hate you. I want to live with my dad."

Anger and hurt welled up inside me. My lips quivered, as I answered, "That can be arranged."

Jamie ran from the living room and out the back door. I stomped into the kitchen, my anger quickly changing to resignation.

The phone rang. I checked the caller ID. It was Dottie. The last thing I needed was her advice, but I couldn't ignore her. My car was in its usual place on the street and she'd know I was home. When I answered, she must have heard the tremor in my voice, because she said, "I'll be right over."

I didn't have time to protest, and in a few minutes, she barged in.

"Rachel, what's happened?" Her mouth pulled into a worried line as she looked around the kitchen. "Has something bad happened to Jamie? Where is the little darling?"

I gritted my teeth. "He's outside and he's fine, but I'm not."

She put her hand on my shoulder. "What's wrong, dear?"

I sniffed. "I'll show you."

I led her to the living room and pointed to the stain. "There."

Dottie stared at the rug and squinted. "What am I supposed to see?"

"That." I squatted, showing her the brown stain while I explained what had happened.

Dottie tilted her head to the side, her curls bouncing. She put her hand to her chin and her mouth twitched at the corners. "Think of it this way, my dear." She tapped her lips. "The change in color adds character and it's definitely an interesting part of the rug's history. You'll have a great story to tell any future guests." She must have thought her comment was funny, because she laughed.

I glared at her. Seeing my irritation, she got serious. "I'd never even notice the mark. It's not visible, but why don't you get the rug professionally cleaned if that will make you feel better?"

"I guess that would probably work." I sniffed.

"Of course," she said, stroking her chin like a learned professor. She paused for dramatic effect, "There is another option. I can get my pistol out of its case and you could shoot the dog at dawn."

She narrowed her eyes and raised her arm. Making a pistol shape with her fingers, she closed one eye, aimed at the place where Scooter had done his business, and fired.

"Pop." The horribly inadequate gunshot sound exploded from Dottie's lips, and her arm kicked back. Bringing the imaginary gun to her lips, she blew the smoke away from the muzzle. Then she lowered her arm and gave me a peculiar expression, with her mouth pulled up to one side. Using a low, growling voice she said, "Partner, that varmint won't be straying into your pasture land no more." Her wild west impression suffered when she couldn't resist laughing at her own performance.

I didn't laugh. My emotions were too raw, what with the incident today and last night's interruption.

I couldn't forget Jamie's remark about hating me and wanting to live with his father. His comment was the straw that broke the camel's back, and his words coiled in my stomach as I realized my gut feeling had been correct. Jamie deserved to be with his father, and I could still make it right.

I'd mail the letter to Walter Sorenson.

Chapter Sixteen

In the couple of weeks that followed Scooter pooping on my silk carpet, Jamie and I hadn't discussed the dog, but I'd watched his efforts to find Scooter a good home. He'd posted handwritten ads on street lampposts, extolling the virtues of the dog. I hoped nobody asked me for a reference regarding Scooter's finer qualities. He was still living in the garage, and Jamie no longer tried to hide the times when he fed or walked him. At least Scooter's last days with Jamie would be full of fond memories.

After lunch, I'd watched Jamie take his bike and go for a ride, with Scooter racing behind him. The pair looked so right together that I'd almost, but not quite, changed my mind—just so I wouldn't have to ruin that sweet picture. I had to remain firm and I kept reminding myself that Scooter and I would never get along. The whole situation would be impossible—*was* impossible.

I'd decided to spend the afternoon doing yard work before the snow came. While I was gathering cones from underneath the huge spruce tree, an oddly shaped white van, or maybe it was an RV, drove up and parked across the street. Hidden from view, I watched as the driver got out.

To my surprise, it was Garrett. What was he doing? Since Elena's death, there hadn't been much activity around the house, and I didn't know whether the owner was planning to sell or rent it again.

Garrett hadn't called me since the near fatal kiss, and I made sure that I kept out of sight. Once he was inside the house, I went around to the other side of the tree, staring at his vehicle and wondering what he was doing at an empty house in the middle of the day.

Not coming up with any answers, I crawled under the tree, gathering needles and debris.

It took me another half hour to get the job completed, but as I surveyed my cleaned-up grass and tidied flowerbeds, I was pleased with my progress. Once I collected my tools, I'd be finished with yard work for the season. I took the rakes, shovel, and broom to the backyard, where I stored them under the step. As I came around the side of the house, I found Garrett standing on the sidewalk. My heart immediately flip-flopped.

"Afternoon," he said, looking amused as his gaze wandered up and down my figure.

I nodded to him, wanting to cover my clothes with my hands, but knowing it would only draw more attention to my appearance. My t-shirt was stained and dirty and my shorts had a rip that ran right up my leg. I wondered if my tiger-striped panties were showing. I combed my hair with my fingers and saw pine needles drop out. I looked at the ground in horror.

Garrett laughed at my expression, but thankfully didn't comment on my organic hair accessories.

"I see you're interested in my van." His scrutiny moved from my head to my dirty garden sneakers, and back up to my t-shirt, where his focus lingered.

I glanced down, horrified. There was a dirt stain on my shirt, right on the tip of one breast that looked just like a nipple. I gulped.

"Would you like to see it?"

I looked at him in shock. "What?" I blinked, and then

suddenly realized what he meant. "Oh, you mean the van?"

He seemed genuinely puzzled. "What else?"

"Um, I wasn't thinking," I answered, flustered. "Of course. Of course, I'd love to see it."

He ran a lazy glance over me, and for a fleeting moment, I thought I saw desire shine in his eyes. A muscle twitched in his jaw, and then he abruptly turned and led the way across the street. I followed.

"The coach door is on the other side." He went around the front of the van and opened the right side of the double doors. "Mind your head."

I ducked and went up the two steps. Inside the van, Garrett stood beside me, looking pleased. I could see why. It wasn't a van really. It was a mobile home.

"This is my baby. It's a van conversion. The back has been extended, and the roof taken off and raised." He put his hand over his head, "See, there's enough room for me to stand up in the kitchen area now, so when I'm doing anything at the sink, I don't have to stoop. It's an older van that I picked up second hand, from a couple who'd only used it gently. The guy had kept it in perfect shape. It's over ten years old, but the engine and transmission are in top condition."

There was a single sink, and under it, a small cupboard. To the right was a three-burner stove, with more storage above it.

"This is compact," I commented. We were standing awfully close. He didn't seem to notice though, and I tried to follow his lead. The van smelled of wood and fresh air, and I had a sudden craving to be in the outdoors.

"On the other side is the bathroom. Switch places with me, so I can let you see it."

I squeezed past him, my arm brushing his soft jacket. I smelled leather. I wanted to rub the material between my fingers and enjoy its softness.

He opened the mirrored bi-fold door and I peered into a tiny bathroom. It had a small, wall-hung sink on the right and a toilet on the left. Attached to the wall near the sink was a shower hose. I wondered how Garrett could maneuver in the cramped space, let alone take a shower.

Garrett saw me scrutinizing the small space. "In case you're wondering, yes, it *is small*, but I rarely use it. You, on the other hand, would fit nicely." He closed the bi-fold, hooking the latch at the top, and then ducked, stepping into the back part of the van. "Watch your head in here."

A single step led into a bedroom. There was no door. On each side of the small room was a single bed, with a two-drawer night table between them.

"Have a seat." Garrett casually indicated the bed across from where he sat, and I perched—not so casually—on the edge of the twin bed, noticing how narrow it was.

"The beds aren't quite as wide as ordinary twin beds, but it's convenient for me, and if I want, I can unscrew the night table between them, use the extra cushions, and make the two small beds into one king-sized bed." He ran his hand over the bedspread.

A twinge of jealousy nipped at me. How many times had he made it into a king-sized bed and how many women had he invited for weekend camping—and other activities?

I couldn't think of anything appropriate to say, so I reverted to my usual trite comment: "It's nice." My mind was racing with other possible responses that were totally inappropriate.

"I'm going out to the mountains tonight." He leaned back with his hands clasped behind his head.

I snuck in a leading question. "Are you meeting with a friend?" I stumbled over the word and managed to correct myself. "Or friends?" I glanced at him, anxious to hear his answer.

"Nothing that exciting. I find it invigorating to breathe

the mountain air. I usually end up hiking. It allows me time to be alone and think."

I was pleased there wasn't a girlfriend involved, so I found myself gushing, "Oh, that sounds wonderful."

With a playful smirk, Garrett gave me another appraising look. "Maybe sometime we can go camping."

"I'd like that," I replied.

The shrewd, assessing glint in his eyes made my stomach give a funny little lurch. He didn't know how much I'd like to camp out with him.

He leaned back on the twin bed and watched me with his eyes half open, as though he were contemplating crawling into bed right now. He was starting to remind me of the overconfident athlete I used to know. Maybe I was reading too much into his steady gaze, though. I needed to regain my composure and disconnect from the warm feelings flowing through my body before I did something foolish. Then I remembered Dottie's advice about offering refreshments. "Would you like to have a cup of coffee?" While I waited for his answer, I studied the floral pattern on the bedspread as if it were an enigma.

"Sounds good to me." He seemed enthusiastic.

I jumped up and bolted from the van, yelling over my shoulder. "I'll get the coffee ready."

Chapter Seventeen

Garrett and I were seated at either end of the nook table. He gave me a penetrating stare that didn't seem at all flirtatious. "I want to discuss Scooter."

All my ideas about Garrett wanting to spend time alone with me crumbled. Now I understood why he'd brought the van and parked across the street. It was a deliberate tactic to pique my interest, and being the curious creature I am, I had fallen right into his trap like a dumb bunny. *Man, he's smooth.*

"Is that the only reason you're here?"

His expression was warm and beguiling, and he slowly shook his head. "I also wanted to see you."

"I see," I said, keeping my tone unemotional. Not knowing how to respond to that admission, I decided to just address his original comment. "Well, you've probably noticed that Jamie's advertising to find a home for Scooter. If he isn't successful soon, I'll check at the local animal shelter and see if they have anybody who'd like a dog."

Garrett frowned, as if he couldn't believe what he was hearing. For a moment, he was looking at me as though I were an evil ogre who'd shot a unicorn. Then the moment passed, and he smiled softly at me.

"Rachel," he murmured my name slowly, as though his voice alone could sway me, "why don't you give the dog another chance?"

I promised myself that I wouldn't be taken in by his good looks and full, kissable lips. I straightened my back and took a fortifying breath. "When I agreed to be Jamie's guardian, I specifically told Mrs. Sorenson that I wouldn't take the dog. That was our deal." I frowned at myself, not too pleased with my choice of the word "deal". It sounded callous.

Garrett flattened his hands on the table as if he were fighting to gain control. "He's a child, Rachel—a little boy who'd be terribly upset if you made him give his dog away. Why else do you think he went to such lengths to hide Scooter?"

I didn't want to be pressured by Garrett. I crossed my arms over my chest, looked to my right, and stared out the window into the backyard. Of course, I saw the garage which made me remember Scooter hiding out there.

I dodged his question and challenged him. "Why'd you bring your van over today? Has Dottie put you up to this?" Her love for Jamie would make her do anything to keep him happy.

"No." He rubbed his jaw, looking frustrated and disapproving. "Rachel ... isn't there some way I can persuade you to change your mind about this?"

"No, but I've got an idea." I leaned forward in an inviting manner, leaning my elbows on the table.

Garrett grinned, as if he were expecting to see the more caring side of me emerge.

"You take the dog. See how you like him messing up *your* house ... or your fancy condo, or wherever it is that you live." I didn't care for the cynicism in my answer, and even less for the disappointment in Garrett's eyes. It was a stupid comment. I had the kid and therefore I *had* to take the dog. I'm sure everyone else would see this as the logical sequence of events

Now I had two people hating me, Jamie *and* Garrett,

and when Dottie found out about my refusal to change my mind, she'd be number three.

Over and over in my mind, I heard Jamie telling me that he hated me, and it stung. I hadn't realized I'd made him so unhappy. The ferocity of his words still shocked me. Someone could have punched me and I think I'd have been less stunned. Before the dog incident, I thought Jamie and I were making progress. It just showed how little I knew about kids.

If Elena Sorenson had known my past history, she'd never have wanted me to take her son. If it were possible, I'd do anything to erase the past and not be at fault for my little brother's tragedy. How would Garrett and Dottie react if they ever found out what I'd done?

They'd all hate me. I'd been making mistakes all along with Jamie, and I wondered if I was making another one now. Could I tolerate a dog?

The truth was, I didn't want him on my property *or* in my house. His fur would be everywhere. I could picture it: great big, fur balls under the furniture, and that doggy smell I detested. I'd never allow Scooter in the living room again.

"What if Scooter continued to stay in the garage?"

Garrett's question surprised me, and I didn't know what to think. So I tried to explain. "With Jamie, I already took on more responsibility than I ever wanted, and I'm not sure I can handle a dog on top of that."

Garrett reached across the table and took my hand. "You can do it, Rachel. I've got faith in you."

His charisma was hard to deny. "I think that all along, the only goal you've had was to persuade me to keep Scooter."

His eyes twinkled and he raised his hands in surrender. "I'm not denying it."

I realized there was more riding on my decision than a boy's love for his dog. I wondered if I was only considering saying yes in order to please Garrett, and if so, if that would be a valid reason. There was one obstacle that had to be overcome either way, though, and I realized I'd better say it right then, before things progressed any further.

"If I agreed to allow Scooter to stay, he *would* have to remain in the garage. If that would be a problem—"

"I don't see *any* problem with Scooter living outside." Garrett nodded. "In fact, I think it's better. From what I've seen, the dog house is well insulated and Scooter's coat is thick and shiny."

I'd never bothered to check Scooter's living accommodations. "Everyone seems to know more about Scooter than I do."

"Get to know Scooter. Show him how much you love him."

"Let's not go too far with the love," I warned. "Scooter is a dog, not a person."

"Are you sure you're really ready to give him another chance? No going back on your decision?" He raised his eyebrow, waiting for my answer.

I sighed, officially relenting. "I'm ready." With Jamie, Garrett, and Dottie all rooting for Scooter, how could I choose to play on the opposing team?

Looking triumphant, Garrett got up from the table. My stomach fluttered over the decision I'd made.

"Jamie's in the yard. Let's go and make him a happy little boy." He put his hand on my back and steered me out of the kitchen, toward the back door.

We saw Jamie and approached him, but before we had time to tell him our news, Dottie appeared. She greeted us with a wink and her usual candidness. "Have you two solved all the world's problems?"

"No, but we've solved one of our own," replied Garrett. He turned to me. "I think Rachel has something she wants to say."

Jamie stood very still and eyed me. Three people watched and waited. I was on stage.

I began in a halting voice. "Well ... I've been rethinking my decision about Scooter."

Jamie looked as if he wanted to hope, but was afraid that—if he did—he might have all his dreams squashed. I realized that this little boy's happiness was what really mattered to me.

Why should I rain on his parade?

I cleared my throat, gearing up to make the big announcement. "The concession I'm going to make comes with conditions." I put up my hand, allowing myself time to think. "I will allow Scooter to stay, if he remains in the garage—"

Before I got to the second condition, Jamie interrupted, blurting out, "Can I take him out for walks and play with him or does he have to stay in the garage *all* the time? Scooter wouldn't be happy in there all the time."

His slumped shoulders and down-turned mouth made me realize how easily I could crush him. *Does he really think I'm so cruel?* "I didn't mean you had to keep the dog in the garage all the time. Of course you can take him for walks and play with him. I wouldn't ever stop you. What I'm trying to say is that Scooter has to *sleep* in the garage."

"Thank you, Rachel." Jamie nodded, but didn't move toward me until Dottie gave him a nudge.

"Show Rachel how you really want to thank her."

After a slight hesitation, he put his arms around me. "Thank you, Rachel," he repeated like a well-trained parrot.

He let go and sidled up to Garrett, who picked him up and hugged him, making me realize how easily jealousy could rear its ugly head.

I guess it wasn't only jealousy I was feeling; it was also the realization that Jamie needed a father—something I couldn't give him.

Chapter Eighteen

After I reversed my decision on Scooter, Jamie appeared more relaxed. His words, "I hate you" still bothered me and I knew such animosity wasn't good for either of us. I hoped to soften his feelings toward me by spending more quality bonding time with him. I'd researched the topic and found a few tips. Tonight I planned on "Engagement through Play." I adapted the idea—encouraging Jamie to tell me about his interests.

We sat in the living room on the hardwood floor, with our backs against the sofa.

Logs hissed and crackled in the fireplace, warming the room. Jamie and I were both in our shorts, pretending it was summer and that we were at the beach.

Outside, the November wind howled. I knew that the next morning I'd be shoveling snow.

"How's school going?" I asked, trying to slip the question in without sounding like I was always checking on him. There hadn't been any phone calls about problems at school, and I was proud of Jamie for adapting to a tough situation.

"We're doing research. Heidi and I are working together and learning how to collect relevant data so when the school fair comes the teacher says we'll be able to work independently on our projects."

It sounded like he was settling into his classes and I was

pleased he mentioned Heidi again. Maybe there was hope for us and Jamie could carry on without Elena. Maybe he could accept me as his guardian.

Jamie changed the subject and chattered about fishing with his dad, and I was determined to show more enthusiasm for his interests.

He had brought in a small green metal box from his room, and lifted it up onto his legs. "My dad got this tackle box for me at a pro shop," Jamie said, opening the top and revealing several compartments.

"What's all this?" I picked up a heavy piece of lead attached to something that looked like a miniature fish.

"It's called a lure. It's a minnow imitation, and fish will bite at it."

"Oh." I tried to picture myself on the banks of a river with a fishing rod in my hand. Definitely not my idea of fun.

"These are floaters or bobbers. When the fish bites, the bobber sinks and you know you've caught something." Jamie's eyes glowed. "I caught a fish with my dad during summer vacation one year. You should have seen it." Jamie stretched his arms out, and I wondered if the fish had really been as big as he remembered.

"These are hooks." Jamie held up a J-shaped fishhook.

It looked like a nasty weapon to me. "Have you ever caught *yourself* with one of these hooks?" An unbidden image of Jamie being gouged entered my mind, making my stomach turn.

"My dad caught his finger with a hook, but he took it out with these." Jamie fished out a pair of pliers. "These are needle-nose pliers, and they're good for extracting fish hooks. That's what my dad says."

There was no doubt about it, Jamie thought his dad was the greatest. His opinion and longing showed with every statement he made. I was glad I'd sent the letter, but if

Walter Sorenson didn't reply in a week or two, I'd get busy searching online and let him know about his son.

I put my arm around Jamie's shoulders and pulled him closer to me. "I hope your dad carries a first aid kit with lots of bandages."

"My dad thinks bandages are for sissies. We went fishing one time and I fell and scraped my knee. I cried, and my dad said that I had to prove I was a man and stop whimpering like a baby."

That sounded awful to me. Almost cruel. "And did you stop crying?" I asked, wondering if my reaction would have been too maternal.

Jamie sat taller "I did." Reaching into the tackle box, he pulled out two tattered photos and dropped them on my lap.

I picked one up and stared at the happy child, who instead of looking at the camera gazed adoringly at his father. They were standing in front of a single log cabin. Walter held his fish by the gills, while Jamie needed both hands to support his substantial-looking catch.

"I went fishing with my dad. We even went there one time in the winter."

In the second photo, Jamie and Walter were standing on the road near a huge snowdrift. One little, brown road sign was readable—just four letters: *W-a-p-i*. In the background, you could see mountains and a lodge. I read the signpost and recognized the name. The mountainous area was known as an all-season area for hiking, fishing and other recreational sports. What I couldn't understand was why Walter hadn't fought for custody rights to have Jamie after Elena died.

I'd managed the first step in the *"Bonding with a Child Guidelines"* so I moved to the next step and tilted my head, touching my cheek against the top of his head. His dark, silky hair was soft and a pang of guilt ran through me. What did I really know about this little boy, who loved fishing, dogs, and most of all, his dad?

I was just settling into a cozy feeling when I felt something soft and squishy squirming just above my knee—a red and yellow worm.

I screamed and jumped to my feet, flinging the thing away. Trembling, I scrubbed at my leg, wanting to get rid of the slimy feel of the worm. It must have crawled out of the tackle box. I shuddered and wished I was wearing shoes. If there were live worms wriggling around the floor, I didn't want to step on them with my bare feet. I scrutinized the floor, but didn't see any.

Jamie tried to stifle his giggles by clamping one hand over his mouth. He scrambled around for a moment, and then raised his other hand, rolling something between his fingers. "This is the worm."

I stopped dancing and squinted at the object.

Jamie rolled the worm back and forth, but it never squished. It took me a few seconds to realize it was a fake.

With my fists on my hips, I glared down at him. "Why'd you do that?"

Jamie shrugged his shoulders innocently. "I wanted to see how far you'd jump."

"Well, now you know."

His mouth tweaked up at the corners. "You're a real good jumper, Rachel."

I gritted my teeth and remembered another important "bonding" rule. *Hang in there with the kid, no matter what he does. You are there for him.* Had the author of those kind words ever have a slimy worm on her bare skin?

Chapter Nineteen

The next afternoon, right after I'd had a late lunch, the doorbell rang. I was surprised and pleased to see Garrett. He wore a khaki parka. The snowflakes that were dotting his dark hair somehow made him look sophisticated and distinguished.

"Come in."

He stomped the snow from his feet and stepped into the foyer, where he removed his boots and took off his jacket. I led the way into the living room and he sat on the sofa. I took the chair facing him. His serious expression made me think that he wasn't here for a social call.

"Was there something you wanted to discuss?" I asked.

Concerned, he leaned forward. "How are things going with Jamie?"

"Better, I think. He showed me his fishing tackle box yesterday. It seems like he's not as shy about opening up to me as he was." To protect my pride, I didn't mention the fake worm or my frenzied dance.

He leaned back, appearing more relaxed. "I'm happy everything is working well. Elena would be so happy."

I nodded, a little disappointed that his only reason for coming was to check on Jamie. I had to put Jamie first, though. I wanted to discuss his need for a father and get Garrett's input.

Seeming to sense my discomfort, and apparently

assuming that I wanted him to leave, Garrett stood up and thrust out his hand, as though we were concluding a business deal. "Once again, I wish to express my thanks for all your work with Jamie."

His words smacked of nothing but business—one person politely thanking another at the conclusion of a meeting. Automatically mimicking his professional behavior, I put out my hand, just as I did at the end of any client consultation.

As our hands touched, Dottie rapped on the door and barged inside. "Hello there!" She didn't have a coat on, and glided into the living room with a plate of cookies in her hand, unaware of the awkward tension hanging in the room.

I let my hand fall to my side and said, "Hi, Dottie."

Ignoring me, she put her hand on Garrett's shoulder. "I don't suppose you were going to visit me, so I'm visiting you. I brought these." She handed him the cookies, and at the same time, steered him out of the room. "Rachel would love to make us some tea, wouldn't you, dear?" I stood with my mouth hanging open. Dottie eyeballed me and jerked her head in the direction of the kitchen, mouthing the words, *"Get with it."*

I followed them. They sat at the nook table while I was busy boiling the water and getting out some herbal tea. Garrett and Dottie were chatting about Jamie.

I envied Dottie's natural gift of the gab. She could chat easily with anyone, especially Garrett. She had the ability to make anyone feel comfortable, whereas I was a lot more at ease and had better rapport with my clients. When Garrett and I were alone, I felt awkward and sensed that my discomfort brushed off on him.

I set the cups on the counter and poured the tea, asking if either Garrett or Dottie wanted cream or sugar. They both said no, and I wondered if my mother had felt this irrelevant to her customers at the diner. I sat at the far end of the table while Dottie passed her plate of cookies to me and continued chatting.

We'd only been sitting a few minutes when Dottie jerked and cupped her hand over her left eye, somewhat melodramatically. "Oh! I've got a problem."

Garrett pushed his chair back and rushed to Dottie's side. "What's the matter?"

"I have something in my eye and it really hurts." She stood and groped along the edge of the table. "Rachel, I need you."

Garrett took Dottie's arm. "Let me help you."

Dottie elbowed him in the ribs, a bit too hard for someone supposedly distracted by terrible pain. "Not you. I want Rachel."

Dottie kept her eye covered, and I helped her toward the kitchen sink.

"No, the bathroom light is better for checking my eye."

I did what she demanded and guided her out of the kitchen, and toward the bathroom. Once we were there, she closed the door, dropped her hands, and eyeballed me, showing no evidence of any problem.

"Would you have offered Garrett a cup of tea?"

"I didn't have a chance. He was in a hurry; now let's see what's wrong with your eye," I said, determined not to let her get away with her charade.

"My goodness, girl, when I arrived, you were shaking his hand. Do you think this is the nineteenth century?"

"He wanted to leave, so I shook his hand."

Dottie rolled her eyes. "With the poor welcome you gave him, no wonder he was planning to escape when I walked in. Another minute and you'd have lost your chance."

"What chance?"

"I've never seen anybody as clueless as you. The guy is

here. What more do you want?"

"Look, he came to check on Jamie. That's why he's here."

Dottie rolled her eyes. "Oh, sure. In the middle of the afternoon when Jamie's at school? Give me a break, girl. Can't you see the guy's interested? Cut him a little slack and show a little enthusiasm."

My whole body stiffened. Dottie's comment was too personal. "Your eye is fine. We can go back."

Dottie wasn't going to be discouraged. "There's a good man in your kitchen, and in case you haven't noticed, he's a dreamboat." Her eyes glazed and she looked like a star-struck teenager. "I'd be shoving you aside if I was twenty years younger. Whereas you ..." She lifted her hands in a gesture of exasperation. "You're killing him with coldness. You made no effort to join in the conversation at the table. I had to keep things going."

I let out a big sigh. "Let's go to the kitchen."

She put her back against the door and held her arms out as if I were going to plow right through her. "I'm not letting you out of here until you tell me what you're going to do."

"I'm thinking," I answered, hoping I'd come up with a plan for encouraging Garrett. I couldn't. "Look, it doesn't matter. He has work to do at the office, so there's nothing I *can* do."

Dottie rolled her eyes. "Give me a break. Ten minutes and you were scaring the guy away."

I defended myself. "He'd been here longer than that by the time you arrived."

"No, he hadn't." She shook her head and her curls bounced. "I set my stopwatch when he drove up, and when I left my house, it was still under ten minutes. It's a good thing I saved you, but you *will* have to do better." She waggled her finger under my nose.

Realizing that Dottie had good intentions, I took a deep breath, and remained calm. She was right; I wanted him to stay longer. "Garrett will wonder if you're all right."

Dottie put her hand up with her palm toward me. "Don't go giving me that pouty look, Rachel McGivney. Jack and I were married for forty-seven years, and I thought we'd celebrate our fiftieth. It wasn't to be. I think about him every day."

Dottie leaned toward me, her expression serious. "Don't you realize that that's what I want for you, Rachel? I want you to share the good and bad times with a man who loves you. That's why I keep encouraging you and Garrett. I wish you'd take my advice."

Her advice struck a nerve, but it was a little more than I expected or wanted.

"Now follow my lead." She strutted down the hall.

By the time we got to the kitchen, I didn't have to say anything to Garrett. Jamie was sitting at the table, chattering away.

Jamie waved a piece of red paper. "Hi, Rachel. Hi, Dottie. This is from school. Guess what? We're having a concert!"

Dottie took the sheet and read it aloud. "All parents, family, and friends are invited to a concert at Maryville Elementary School on Thursday night."

I frowned. "That's only two days away. The school certainly didn't give us much notice."

"It's been in my backpack," Jamie admitted, as he stared at the floor.

I wasn't going to give him a lecture on the necessity of promptly delivering notices from the school, so I dropped the matter.

Dottie clapped her hands. "This is fantastic! We can all go to the concert. You will come, won't you?" She tilted her head and batted her eyes at Garrett.

"Wouldn't miss it." He ruffled Jamie's hair and said, "Walk with me so we can talk."

Garrett said goodbye. After he and Jamie left the kitchen, Dottie smirked. "Children have perfect timing."

Chapter Twenty

The concert night came in a big hurry. After Jamie brought the invitation home, he'd told me he needed a white shirt, dark pants—not jeans—and if possible, dress shoes.

After school, we'd gone shopping and bought everything on his list.

The night of the concert, Jamie had to get to school an hour before it started, and Garrett had offered to pick us up, saying that he wanted a good seat.

Much to my surprise, a lot of other parents had arrived early too, and had already taken the front seats. The floor of the auditorium was filled with chairs.

We were back six rows, but I still had a good view of the stage. The dark green stage curtains were closed, and people chatted. A feeling of excitement filled the air. Coats hung over the backs of chairs which were placed close together.

I sat on a metal chair, sandwiched between Dottie and Garrett. Both of them had taken off their coats and I could feel their bodies pressing against me. I wiggled closer to Dottie, and in doing so, I rubbed against Garrett's leg. A funny feeling settled in the pit of my stomach.

Garrett stared at me with a steady, disarming look, and I diverted my gaze, anxiously searching the program for Jamie's name. I found it. He was listed as part of a duet with another boy, whose name I didn't recognize.

"Isn't this fun?" Dottie leaned in front of me, directing her comment to Garrett. "I can hardly wait to see our child on stage. He's such a darling."

Garrett nodded, and with a tone of pride, he said, "He's a good kid."

"You get along well with Jamie," I said. The question I really wanted to ask him was why he wasn't Jamie's guardian.

His mouth quirked into a smile. "I've always liked kids."

"You didn't want any of your own?" I asked.

He shrugged, and was saved from answering when Dottie pushed her chair closer to mine.

"I want to have a better view of our boy," she explained.

The lights dimmed, indicating that the program was about to begin. I craned my neck as the teacher sat down at the piano. Two boys emerged from behind the stage curtain and my heart beat faster as I watched Jamie and the other boy stand in front of the microphone. Dressed in white shirts, dark pants, and red vests, they reminded me of a pair of angels. I reminded myself that looks can be deceiving.

The boys glanced at the teacher. She nodded and played the introduction. I recognized the music after the first bar. It was an old song about a child searching for love. I swallowed against the sudden tightness in my throat, and stared straight ahead, trying not to blink.

The words Jamie sang haunted me. Was he looking for the love I'd failed to provide?

The second line in the song spoke of the loss of a mother. Jamie's voice quivered and I sat rigid, hoping he wouldn't falter. Out of the corner of my eye, I saw Garrett's serious expression. I would never expect Jamie to get over the loss of his mother, but I promised myself I'd continue to make more of an effort, no matter what he said or did.

The words at the end of the song rang with the innocence of a child. I bit my tongue, but couldn't hold back a sniffle. Was Jamie thinking of his father? Did he want to be with him more than with me? I would understand perfectly. After my dad left, I'd always longed to see my biological father, but never had. A few years ago, when I'd read in the newspaper that he had died, a part of me died too.

Once the song was over, I couldn't stop the surge of pride that was filling me. The audience burst into applause and yelled, "Bravo!" for my Jamie. I sat in a contented glow. *My* Jamie. I dried my eyes with the back of my hand. I didn't know he could sing. There were so many things about him that I needed to learn.

Dottie patted me on the leg. "Wow, our boy sure can sing. Isn't he a darling?"

A sudden tightness gripped me and I thought my chest would burst. I could still see Elena Sorenson, sitting in her living room chair at the mistletoe party, and kissing the top of Jamie's head as she smiled at me. I could only hope that, at this moment, she was smiling down on us, proud of her son and happy with her decision.

Chapter Twenty-one

The concert ended around nine o'clock and we waited for Jamie outside the gym. Around us, parents and kids hugged, and I started to think that school concerts weren't such a bad idea—if your parents actually attended.

Jamie appeared. "You sang beautifully. I'm so proud of you." I patted him on the head and then, remembering that showing affection would help Jamie open up, I hugged him and he hugged me tighter.

Once we were settled in the car, with our seat belts fastened, Garrett turned to Jamie and Dottie, who were sitting in the back seat. "Since Jamie earned it, where can I take you all for a treat?"

"I know just the place," Dottie answered, before I could get my mouth in gear. "We'll go home, and while Jamie gets into his pajamas, and Rachel makes the tea, I'll pick up some baking."

It was a good idea. If we went straight home, Jamie would get to bed earlier and settle more quickly. If she was volunteering the pastries, I'd supply the tea.

When we arrived home, I was still feeling a warm glow from Jamie's performance. He'd done us all proud, but I realized that he still longed for his mom, and that I could never take her place.

"Rachel, can I say goodnight to Scooter?" asked Jamie, as he opened the car door.

"Yes." I'd relented about keeping the dog, so I wasn't sure why I still harbored ill feelings toward him. I guessed I just couldn't forget my beautiful silk rug. I'd taken it to the cleaners to see if they could gently clean it. They reassured me that I would never know there had been a stain. I didn't think I'd ever forget the incident, but I was trying to put it behind me.

"I'll have the baking over in a flash," said Dottie, as she got out and strode toward her house.

Watching her, I admired her energy and hoped I'd have as much enthusiasm when I got older.

Once Garrett and I were in the house, he helped me with my coat. His fingers brushed the nape of my neck and his hand rested on my shoulder. My heart thumped.

"I enjoyed tonight," he said.

Before I had a chance to respond, I heard a scuffle from the back door and Jamie's voice. "You wait here."

As I entered the kitchen, I saw Scooter sheepishly peering around the corner of the back hall. I got within a few feet of him and pointed my finger right near his nose. "Sit," I commanded.

He obeyed, his big brown eyes pleading with me to like him, and his hindquarters wiggling back and forth. "You know you're not supposed to be in here, so don't give me the blameless look."

Scooter must have taken my words as a sign of encouragement. In an instant, he was on his feet and rubbing his shoulders against my leg, with his tail swishing the air. I wasn't sure if his actions were a sign of friendship or something else. He hadn't proved he was trained.

I wanted to ask Jamie why he'd brought Scooter into the back hall, but he was standing with the dog's water bowl in his hand. "Scooter can't drink this." He tilted the bowl so I could see the layer of ice at the top.

I imagined Jamie considered this another black mark

against me, expecting the dog to drink frozen water.

"I'll get some fresh water." I took the bowl, and passed Garrett, who'd now come into the back hall. When I returned from the kitchen, Jamie and Garrett were on either side of the dog, with Garrett rubbing Scooter's back. The dog gazed at the wall with a dreamy expression as if he were being treated to a massage at the best spa in town.

The three of us stood around Scooter for a long moment, and I was struck by the absurdity of two adults and one child fawning over a dog as if he were an endangered species. "I think his highness has had enough attention from the three of us."

Before I could walk away, Garrett put his hand on my arm, and with a convincing look that rivaled the dog's for sincerity, he said, "Wait, Rachel. Touch Scooter's coat."

I grimaced. "Why would I do that? He sheds."

Garrett rubbed his hand through the dog's fur. "It's thick and shiny."

I edged toward the kitchen and said over my shoulder. "Good. I'm glad. In the spring, we'll give him a haircut, and shear him like a sheep." I wanted to add, *now let me out of here and get the dog back where he belongs*, but Garrett had more to say.

"Sheepdogs prefer colder weather. He's healthier than I ever remember him being when I visited Elena. Truthfully, he was getting too fat and she always had the heat up very high. I think you've done Scooter a favor."

Chapter Twenty-two

Shortly after Jamie went to bed, Dottie announced that she was going to be on her way as well.

Garrett pushed his chair back and stood. "I'll see you to the door and walk you home."

She waved him aside. "Uh-uh. You sit. I want to talk to Rachel."

In the vestibule, I helped Dottie with her coat. She cupped her hand over her mouth and whispered, "This is your chance. The kid's in bed and you've got the dreamboat all alone. The ball is in your court."

"I know." I tried to mask my anxiety over finally being alone with Garrett. "Thanks for bringing the treats."

She wasn't going to be sidetracked. "If you drop the ball this time, all my hopes and dreams for you will be shattered."

I considered what she had said. As I closed the door, I got a shot of inspiration. I'd kissed Garrett at the mistletoe party. We were consenting adults. Why shouldn't I make it easier for him to kiss me again? Heaven knows, I wanted it. *Besides, who am I to shatter an old woman's dreams?* I strolled into the kitchen, pumped with new-found confidence.

Garrett was sitting at the table. I rested my elbows on the counter, cupped my chin in my hands, and tried to appear relaxed, even though my heart was racing. "Perhaps we'd be more comfortable in the living room," I said, in what I hoped was an enticing manner.

He must have taken that as the right opening for his next statement, because he got up and stood on the other side of the counter, with a wrinkled brow. "Are you and I *ever* going to be comfortable with each other?"

It wasn't the reply I'd been hoping for, and the honesty of it caught me by surprise. My jaw slackened at his frank appraisal. I fumbled for my next words. "I don't know." I shrugged and couldn't look at him, so I let my gaze wander, hoping he'd fill in the silence. When he didn't, I added, "I'm not at ease with ... company of the opposite sex." At least not the company of one man in particular, who I was afraid would compare me to every other woman he'd dated, exposing me as clumsy and inexperienced.

His serious expression softened, and he laughed. "Dottie makes things awkward for both of us. She's been pushing us together since you stumbled into the living room at Elena's mistletoe party."

I nodded. There was no point in denying it. I'd hoped he hadn't noticed Dottie's blunt attempts to force us together, but since he had, I spilled the truth. "It's really embarrassing. I can't stop her. She gives me one lecture after another, and she's always telling me to stop acting like I've just stepped out of the nineteenth century."

His face was drawn into a mock frown, but his voice was like liquid silk. "When I picture women from that era, I imagine elegance and grace." He raised an eyebrow. "What's wrong with being a little old-fashioned?"

Wanting him to understand more, I rambled on. "I feel as if I've missed the boat somehow. I'm so far behind the women of today and ... and the way they act so freely. I honestly don't know what to do." I raised my hands. Without telling him directly, I wanted him to understand that intimacy with a man had me worried.

He leaned over the counter until we were face to face—

our lips almost touching. The fresh scent of his cologne encircled me as he brushed the back of his hand over my cheek. A shiver danced across my skin.

"I find you both refreshing and endearing." His eyes darkened. "Not like some other women I've met. I've had my fill of them." He touched his lips to my forehead and I stretched, cursing the counter between us as I tried to get closer.

He put his hands on my shoulders, smiling gently, and pushing me away. "I do have to get into the office early tomorrow morning, though." He straightened and walked through the dining room toward the front door.

I followed behind him, trying to understand what had gone wrong and hide my disappointment and embarrassment over my clumsy, failed attempt to put the moves on him.

"I'll see you on the weekend," he said, glancing casually over his shoulder as he left.

As I watched him go to his car, I could hear Dottie saying that I'd dropped the ball.

Again.

Chapter Twenty-three

The following Saturday morning, I was lying in bed, making plans for the day. After I finished seeing a client this morning, I'd take a walk with Jamie, or if he wanted, we could go to the sports arena and play in the pool. I wasn't a good swimmer, but I enjoyed the wave machine. We could also try the slide. Barreling down the chute and zooming out into the water would be great fun, even if I had to dog paddle to the side.

Jamie flushed the toilet in the bathroom and I wondered if he'd come to see me. I waited, hoping, like some child who waits for a gift to be delivered.

My thoughts shocked me. What was getting into me? I was comparing Jamie to a gift? I laughed at how my feelings toward him had changed.

He rapped on the door. "Rachel. Can I come in?"

"Of course."

The door banged and vibrated against the stopper and I bit my tongue to keep from reminding him to be gentle.

He plunked onto the edge of the bed. "Can I go out and play with Scooter?"

The enthusiasm in his voice and the sparkle in his eye caused a lump in my throat. I took his hand and for a minute, he looked surprised. Then he grinned and I wanted to hug him, as I'd seen Elena do. I still wasn't comfortable with pulling him toward me, though, or giving him a kiss. I wanted to respect his comfort level.

"Why don't you go and feed Scooter and then come in for breakfast? After you've eaten, you can play with Scooter in the backyard while I tidy up." I didn't mind them racing around the backyard. A few patches of snow were on the ground and my flowerpots had been safely stored under the back steps.

His eyes brightened. "Sure, Rachel." He slid off the bed and thumped toward the kitchen.

I complimented myself. Jamie and I were definitely making progress. I know I'd been touched, and at the same time saddened, by the words in the song he'd sung the other night, but he didn't seem sad this morning. I didn't want to be too impressed with my progress, but I figured I had to be doing something right with Jamie, or he wouldn't be so spontaneous and happy.

As I glanced in the dresser mirror, though, a little voice was reminding me: *Jamie is happy because he's got his dog. Don't put your elbow out of joint giving yourself too big a pat on the back.*

I got dressed, and after breakfast I stood in the kitchen, with Jamie beside me, while I talked on the phone with Dottie. "Jamie says that he wants to play outside in the yard while I'm away. Can you keep an eye on him?"

Dottie agreed. I nodded to Jamie, indicating that she had okayed his plan. He grinned.

Before I left, we reviewed the safety list although I knew he'd be perfectly secure in the backyard. It was fenced, and Dottie was keeping her eye on him from her kitchen window. For my own peace of mind, I went over the directions anyway.

"I'll lock the front door, but there's no need to lock the back one with you and Scooter playing in the yard. If you need to come inside, you won't need your key. Now, promise me you won't bring Scooter in here." I had to stop myself from waving my finger and giving a lecture. There was still so much I had to learn about children, but I was discovering that preaching and finger shaking didn't cut it with the modern kid.

Jamie put up his hand like a witness testifying in court. "I promise."

I gave him a quick kiss on the forehead. A picture of Elena kissing Jamie flashed into my mind as I was brushing his hair with my fingers, and a rush of affection coursed through my body. Impulsively, I hugged him. "That's my boy," I mumbled.

He stiffened and I let go, regaining my composure. "You go out and play. I'll be back by lunch time."

"Okay, Rachel." He raced out of the room. I don't know what got into me, but I wanted to run after him to give him one last big hug. He disappeared so fast, I missed the chance.

Chapter Twenty-four

A few hours later, I arrived home. After I'd finished with my clients, I'd picked up some peanut butter, bananas, and apples for Jamie. He was the typical kid, quite content with simple food.

I parked and carried the bag of groceries up the stairs. I liked the crispness in the air. The sky was overcast, with a forecast calling for snow, but I figured Jamie and I would have time to go out for a walk and be back home before the flurries started.

I was pulling the key out of my purse when Dottie opened the door. I expected that she and Jamie were playing some board game they both loved, but Dottie's anguish crushed the pleasant thought and a wave of terror washed over me. "What's wrong?"

Her lips quivered. Afraid she'd faint, I dropped my groceries on the floor, and took her by the arm, ushering her to the sofa.

Confusion spilled over me. I looked around. Nothing seemed out of place, but a certain boy was nowhere to be seen. "What's happened?"

She looked up at me, her face white and pinched. "It's Jamie ... Jamie's gone."

My stomach knotted. "What do you mean *gone*? Gone where? He can't just disappear!" I asked, refusing to give in to the fear that threatened to control my body. "He's got to be here someplace."

I glanced around the living room as if I expected to see him jump out from a hiding place.

"Did he tell you he was leaving?"

Dottie shook her head and whimpered into her handkerchief. "I've looked for him nonstop, but I can't find him."

I told myself that I had to be rational and keep my fears at bay. There must be some logical explanation. Jamie couldn't just vanish without a trace. "We'll find him," I reassured Dottie. I was beginning to feel light-headed.

If he'd taken off for a bike ride without telling Dottie, I was going to ground him—no compromising. A week? No. A month? I didn't know for how long. Another fear squirmed inside me, and I choked on my breath. What if Jamie really was missing? "Jamie," I yelled. "If you're hiding, it's time to stop the game and come out." But even as I said the words, I reminded myself that Jamie had never hidden before. It wasn't a game he played.

I rushed to the backyard and yelled, but there was no answer. Looking through the lattice fence, I scanned Dottie's yard. He wasn't there either. My heart thumped. I ran into the house and shouted, "Dottie! Dottie, where are you?"

"In here," she called from the back bedroom. I ran down the hall.

Dottie was on her hands and knees checking under Jamie's bed. She lifted her head. "I wondered if he was hiding."

I backed out of the bedroom and glanced into the bathroom. A small piece of yellow paper, which was propped up between the taps and the back-splash tile, caught my attention. *What's that doing there?*

I picked it up with the intent of throwing it in the wastebasket, but my stomach dropped when I recognized the printing. The note read:

> *Hi Rachel,*
> *My daddy came*
> *Went for a ride*
> *Jamie*

He'd added a little happy face after his name.

My stomach tightened into a hard, little knot when I realized that Jamie had left the sticky note in the bathroom—the first place I always went, after being away, to wash my hands. It was a good plan, but the tiny note had dropped behind the taps—easy for Dottie to overlook. She probably hadn't stepped into the bathroom. The room was small, and even if Jamie had decided to hide in the bathtub, she could have seen him from the doorway.

"Dottie," I whispered, paralyzed by a horrible churning in my stomach.

"What's wrong, Rachel?"

I handed her the note.

She frowned. "I don't understand. What's this about his daddy?" She slapped at the piece of paper. "Why would he take Jamie? Who is this man? Is he dangerous? You've got to phone the police!"

"It's all right, Dottie. Jamie is with his dad and he'll be safe." A little voice niggled in my head. *Kids have been kidnapped by their own parent.* I didn't want to believe this could happen. Did Walter kidnap Jamie because he had gotten my letter? In my annoyance with Jamie, I had invited Walter to take his son. No, that wasn't accurate. I'd suggested getting together and discussing Jamie. Walter needed to know that Jamie still loved him and my letter must have triggered Walter's desire to visit.

"I think I might know where he is." I went to my laptop and did an online search for Walter's phone number, and when I found it, I punched it into my cell phone. When I didn't get an answer, I said, "I'm going to wait a few minutes and try the number again. Walter might be in some area where the signal is blocked." I remembered when I'd been in a hotel and hadn't been able to get service until I got closer to an outside wall.

While I was waiting I did a reverse address search for Walter, the same method I'd used when I'd mailed the letter to Walter. Hoping to buoy Dottie's confidence I held up my phone. "I've got Walter's address and if Jamie isn't home soon, I'll drive over there and check if that's where they are." I tried to sound rational in order to keep Dottie calm. I put the phone on the coffee table.

Dottie glanced nervously at it. "Why don't you phone Garrett and ask him what to do?"

"There's no need to alarm Garrett, Jamie has to be someplace safe." Only I didn't know the location and every minute Jamie wasn't with us increased my anxiety.

"If you won't do it, then I will." She scooped up the phone. "What's his number?"

"It's really not necessary." I put out my hand for her to give me the phone.

She pressed the phone to her chest. "I've got a bad feeling about Jamie. If you don't tell me Garrett's number, I'll go home and look it up."

"Okay." I took the phone from her and selected the number. It rang several times and when Garrett finally picked up, I explained the situation to him. He said he'd check Walter's residence and then drop by my house. In the meantime I'd continue trying to get hold of Walter.

While Dottie and I waited for news from Garrett, I ran outside to check on Scooter. In my panic, I hadn't considered the dog. To my relief, I found that he'd disappeared too. *At least, he isn't alone with the man. Scooter will protect him if he needs to.*

Twenty minutes later, Garrett arrived and I showed him the note from Jamie.

"Now, do we phone the police?" Dottie sat on the sofa, pressing her knuckles against her teeth.

I sat beside her, remembering the last time I'd answered questions from a police officer. For the past thirty-one years, I'd fought to keep my horrible secret hidden, but I'd made another potentially fatal mistake by writing the letter to Walter. And in mailing it, I had sealed Jamie's fate. History was repeating itself. I was destroying another little boy's life.

Looking confused, Garrett said, "Elena and Walter were divorced two or three years ago. I don't understand Walter's sudden interest in Jamie. According to what Elena said, he never showed much before, so what's changed?"

I couldn't feign ignorance any longer. It wasn't going to be easy, but I had to explain. I steeled myself for the chastising that was sure to come. After taking a deep breath, I confessed quickly, before I lost the nerve. "I know why Walter took Jamie."

Dottie's mouth dropped open.

Garrett's eyes narrowed and he studied me.

I explained how I'd written and mailed the letter to Walter after Jamie said that he hated me and wanted to be with his dad.

I saw shock and fear on Dottie's face, as she wiped her eyes with a handkerchief. Garrett sat rigid, and in his expression, I thought I could read condemnation and disappointment.

Their total silence pressed in on me, threatening to suffocate me. "I told you I wouldn't be a suitable guardian for Jamie." My feeble excuse couldn't ease the gnawing emptiness in my gut or justify my actions.

Garrett bowed his head and tapped his index finger against his lips.

Dottie stared out the window. Her shoulders sagged, and she seemed to have aged ten years in the last hour. "I'm so sorry, Rachel. I'd never put our boy in harm's way." Her chin trembled. "You have to know how horrible I feel about neglecting my duty and leaving Jamie alone. I should have been here with him."

I bit my lips in an unsuccessful attempt to keep the tears away. I went to Dottie and put my arms around her. "You're not to blame. Jamie's with his dad. He'll be okay."

Garrett tapped my shoulder. "I think it's time for Dottie to go home." His practical manner didn't completely mask his concern.

I let my arms drop to my sides and wiped my tears with the back of my hand. "Jamie's going to be okay, Dottie." I had to convince her, even if I questioned my own words.

"Of course, Rachel. Of course." She patted my arm with listless conviction.

Garrett helped Dottie get home. I watched him carefully guide her along the sidewalk until they turned into her front yard and I couldn't see them anymore.

Garrett would be back soon. I dreaded his disapproval. How could I make him understand without telling him everything? I had a few minutes to try to compose myself before he got back. I sat on the sofa, trying to decide what to say. Garrett returned before I even had time to think.

He stormed back into the living room. "You have lots of explaining to do." He shot me a scouring look, the fear he was feeling for Jamie clearly turning to anger and frustration. "What part of Elena's decision not to have Jamie go with her ex-husband didn't you understand?"

My guilt gnawed at me and put me on the defensive. I raised my head. "Well, what part of 'I wouldn't make a good guardian' couldn't *you* get through *your* thick head? You and Elena pestered me until I finally gave in!" My own words stunned me. I thought we'd been making progress.

There was nothing else for me to say in my defense, so I clamped my mouth shut and glared at him.

He dropped his gaze. Not saying a word, he sat in the chair opposite me, his eyes downcast. When he raised his head and looked at me, the anger was gone, but I could see lines of sorrow etched on his face. "I didn't realize you were so against Jamie."

His words stung. "I wasn't *against* Jamie! And I'm *certainly* not anymore!" I protested. Once again, I'd been proved unfit. *How many times am I going to make a mistake with a child's life?* "I didn't think—"

"That's the problem!" He interrupted. "You *didn't* think!" His sharpness stunned me. We sat in silence for a long moment. I could see him taking deep breaths, attempting to calm down. "I'm sorry. Snapping at each other is not going to solve anything. I'm sure we're both just upset by what's happened."

After another long moment, I forced myself to ask the underlying question that was haunting me. "Did Walter abuse Jamie?"

"No. There was no physical abuse of Elena or Jamie. Walter just wasn't interested in Jamie. Elena used the word 'indifferent'."

"I don't understand why he wouldn't *love* Jamie."

"I've never met Walter, so I have no idea. Apparently, the fighting between them came to a head two years ago when Elena and Walter divorced. There was no squabbling over their son. It was simple. Elena was given sole custody of Jamie. Walter didn't demand any visitation rights. In fact, he waived all rights to ever see Jamie again."

His words stabbed my heart and I recoiled in horror at Walter's coldness. "No weekends? No holidays to be with his son?" What kind of father never wanted to see his child again, and then suddenly decide to pick him up as if he were taking him for a Sunday afternoon drive? What kind of uncaring man had I contacted?

Garrett paced and combed his fingers roughly through his hair. "I made a big mistake. I've done something a lawyer isn't supposed to do."

Warning bells went off in my head. As far as I'd seen, Garrett was a stickler for rules. I couldn't imagine him breaking the law or jeopardizing his career for any reason.

Noting my baffled stare, he clarified, "I'm supposed to offer guidance, not dictate to my clients."

"I'm still not following you."

He stopped pacing. "Do you *ever* think to offer a fellow a cup of coffee or tea? It might make us both feel better." He smiled and I realized he was trying to lighten the situation.

Chapter Twenty-five

My stomach ached from the tension of what Garrett was going to tell me. I wanted to urge him to tell me quickly, so I would know the extent of the misery I'd caused, but I had to wait. He'd tell me in his own good time and I'd try to be patient. I went into the kitchen.

While the tea was steeping, I dumped some cookies on a plate and placed them in the center of the table along with some napkins. Garrett took a couple and munched on them.

I was ready to scream, so I sat at the far end of the table and blundered into conversation, expressing personal opinions I'd vowed I'd never say.

"I don't know why Elena picked me to be Jamie's guardian. I didn't know her—not even her first name. I didn't like her child and I *certainly* wasn't a big fan of Scooter. Did she ever really explain why?" After a long moment of silence, I glared at him—my anxiety overpowering my good judgment. "You're not answering me."

He covered his face with his splayed hand and I could hardly hear his words. "I gave some very bad advice. A mistake on my part."

"What are you talking about? Instead of talking in riddles, why don't you tell me what you mean?"

"Elena Sorenson did *not* pick you to be her son's guardian."

My breath caught in my throat. I didn't believe him. There was some mistake. I had to make sure everything was registering correctly in my mind. "How can you say that? I *told* you, she invited me over, asked me about the guardianship, and at first I said 'no'. Eventually I gave in and agreed to do it. What part of that don't you understand?"

He let out a bit of a sigh and stared hard at the floor. Minutes passed before he lifted his head. "I understand it all too well. But I went against everything I tell young lawyers not to do."

"What do you mean? What have you done? I'm the one who wrote the letter to Walter, with my return address on it, so he'd know where to find Jamie. I'm the person who's responsible."

Garrett shook his head. "None of this would have happened if I hadn't allowed my heart to rule my head."

Tears stung my eyes. Every insult and brush-off I'd endured in high school reared its ugly head. I remembered one night when I'd been helping Mom in the diner. Some of Garrett's teammates had come in, and one of the guys, after shuffling back and forth nervously, approached me and asked me out on a date. Knowing that my mom wouldn't permit me to date him, I refused, perhaps too hastily. The football player was irked and his flirty attitude changed to a jeer as he informed me that he would only date me for one reason anyway. There were a lot better, cuter choices and he could have his pick of any of them. Other insults came tumbling back into my mind, but I couldn't let them overcome me. I forced myself to straighten my backbone and look directly at Garrett.

"Since when have you allowed your heart to rule?" I asked.

"Since your name was put on the list."

"What list?" I rubbed my temples, trying to ease the pounding.

"If you can sit without interrupting me for a few minutes, I'll tell you."

"All right." I twisted my hands and eventually decided to sit on them.

"Elena Sorenson gave me a list of names ... of people she was considering as possible guardians for Jamie."

"A list?" I pulled my hands from under my legs and placed my elbows on the table, clasping my hands together and pressing my thumbs against my lips. My heart was thumping. Despite my misgivings about taking Jamie, I'd been proud that Elena had picked me over everybody else. But if what Garrett said was true, I was only one of many names.

"What about the other people? Where was I on the list?" I had some horrible feeling that my crime of so many years ago, the one I'd worked so hard to forget, was coming back to haunt me. What I'd done to my brother had been terrible enough. Now, once again, I'd shirked my duty with another little boy.

"You weren't at first, I suggested you. Her ex-husband wasn't on it either."

His answer surprised me. I pressed my throat to stifle a gasp. "Didn't it seem reasonable that the child should just go to his father?"

"I made that suggestion too, but Elena was adamant that Jamie not be with Walter."

I shifted and glanced at the clock on the wall. "It's been over an hour," I said. "You'd think Walter would have brought Jamie home by now." My eyes and throat stung. I walked to the sink and poured myself a glass of water. The cool drink eased my dry throat, but did nothing to ease the torment in my mind.

I picked up the phone and dialed Walter's phone

number again but received no connecting signal.

"Do you have any idea where Walter might have taken Jamie?" Garrett stood on the other side of the raised bar, looking tired and frustrated.

I shook my head and then I remembered. "Jamie showed me a photo." I raced to his bedroom and found the tackle box and removed the photo. Back in the nook, I showed the photo to Garrett.

He studied it. "I think I know this place. It's in the mountains ... and there's even a lake nearby. They wouldn't go fishing now, but there's a lodge in the area and I think it stays open in the winter. It's a long shot, but Walter might have driven there."

I was grasping at straws. "We have to search. I can't bear staying here any longer. We have to find Jamie and bring him home."

Chapter Twenty-six

Garrett said he didn't mind driving to the mountains. The van had snow tires and was equipped for winter travel. Knowing the weather could be much colder, I got my heavy coat, knit cap, mittens, and boots.

"What if Jamie comes back home and you're not here?" Garrett's logical question jarred me. In my anxiety, I hadn't been thinking straight.

"I'll call Dottie and ask her to come over. She can get me on the cell phone if Jamie gets home before we do."

Once we were in the van, I settled into the captain's chair on the passenger side. The streets were clear and there wasn't much snow on the boulevards, but I knew it could be a lot different in the mountains, where the packed snow would be deeper and the temperature colder.

I tried not to fidget. It was a long shot looking for a kid in the mountains, but I couldn't sit at home. I felt like one of the parents I'd seen in documentaries, who drive around the streets at night looking for their missing teenagers.

"Rachel." Garrett sounded amused. "Stop biting your lips; you're going to hurt yourself."

"Oh, sorry," I muttered. I hadn't realized I'd been doing it.

"There's no sense in beating yourself up. Now take this map and see if there are any names that trigger a memory of something Jamie might have said."

Garrett pulled a map from a storage compartment. I unfolded it and spread it out on my lap, peering at the names.

After a few minutes, Garrett asked, "Do you see any places you think Jamie might have mentioned?"

"I'm not sure. There was a place he mentioned a couple of times, where he used to go fishing, but he couldn't pronounce it. He said that it sounded like '*Minna*' something, but with more syllables at the end. When he couldn't come up with it, I remember laughing and telling him we'd just call it Minnow Lake."

Garrett looked sober. "The closest name I can think of is Lake Minnewapi, which *is* in the mountains. It'll take a while to get there, but we should make it before dark."

The main highway was well maintained, with no icy patches, and every time another vehicle came into sight, I swiveled my head to check for a man and small child, but the traffic was light.

"Why don't you try to rest for a few minutes? I'll be on the lookout."

"Okay." I sniffed and wiped the sleeve of my jacket over my eyes.

"Relax, Rachel. I'm sure Jamie is safe with Walter and we'll find them."

He put his right hand over my interlocked hands. The warmth from it seeped into my fingers. "It's going to be all right," he reassured me.

I ended up holding his hand between both of mine, wishing I could believe him. I stared out the window at the blackened snow, which had been plowed to the side of the road, and beyond it to the evergreens.

After what seemed like forever, we took the cut-off to Deer Run Lodge.

"Good. It *is* open." Garrett pointed out the window toward the tall, brown "open" sign, "Most of these lodges are closed for the winter season, but I thought Deer Run Lodge stayed open for a few guests."

His words encouraged me. We turned onto the secondary road. It had been plowed, but there were high drifts on the shoulders. The road twisted and looped, with any full view of the mountains being blocked by tall evergreens covering the landscape. I glanced at my watch. We'd only been on this road for twenty minutes. It felt longer.

Garrett eased off the gas and we rounded another curve. A smaller brown sign that was jutting out of the snow caught my attention, but we were past it before I could see what was on it.

"Would you mind going back?"

He slowed the van. "Why?"

"I just saw a sign. I want to look at it again."

Without saying anything, he stopped and backed up to where I'd seen the sign.

Poking out of the snowdrift at the side of the road was a sign post with the words "Lake Minnewapi" and an arrow pointing to the right. "Let's take this road. I'm sure that's the sign in the photo of Jamie and his dad." The pitch of my voice was higher than normal, as a wave of excitement and fear rattled through me. Had we at last found some clue to Jamie's whereabouts?

"Look! There's a set of tire tracks!" I pointed to the marks in the snow. "Maybe it means Walter took Jamie this way." I put my fist to my mouth and gnawed on my knuckle.

"We'll give it a try."

Although the road had been roughly plowed, there was still snow on it. The drifts at the side were four or five feet high.

"The tracks look fresh." I grasped at any hope of finding Jamie.

"Well, to be honest, it hasn't snowed recently or melted. The tracks could have been made an hour ago or yesterday." Garrett's reply didn't give me any confidence.

I wanted to believe they were recent, and that we'd find Jamie with his father at the end of this trail. It was possible, but not particularly likely. More worries rushed into my mind. Were we on a wild goose chase to the middle of nowhere? Why hadn't I stayed at home waiting for Jamie to return?

The van bumped and slipped over icy patches and Garrett swore under his breath as he fought with the wheel. The vehicle slid to the left. I bit my tongue, so that my gulping wouldn't give away my uneasiness.

The tires crunched on the snow and I wondered how long ago the tracks we were following had been made. The engine strained as the road got steeper.

"We'll drive for ten or fifteen minutes more, but if we don't find anything. I'll have to back out."

I tasted bile in the back of my throat. I kept quiet, hoping we would find Jamie in the next few minutes.

"I don't want to be on this road when it gets dark." Tension sounded in Garrett's voice.

I nodded. I didn't want to be slipping and sliding in the darkness either. In the winter, the sun set behind the mountains not much later than mid-afternoon. It could be dark in an hour. We rounded a bend in the road and my chest tightened. We'd reached the end of the trail. A black car was parked with its nose pointing into a snowdrift. To the right, a path had been packed down in the snow, leading to a small cabin. Smoke puffed out of the chimney.

Were Walter and Jamie there?

Garrett pulled the van into the cramped space to the left of the car. There wasn't enough room for either of us to get out of the cab, so we used the coach doors.

I edged sideways between the vehicles, following

Garrett around the back of the car. I placed my hand on the trunk and the coldness bit through my gloves, making me shiver. It had clearly been parked for a while.

The glowing light from the cabin window buoyed my spirits as I followed in Garrett's footsteps. Was this the end of our search? Had we found Jamie?

Chapter Twenty-seven

G arrett stepped onto the covered porch that ran across the entire front of the wooden cabin. He pounded on the door and yelled, "Mr. Sorenson, are you in there?"

I stood on the porch beside Garrett. While we waited, I shifted from one foot to the other and wiggled my hands, trying to ease the coldness in my fingers.

There was no reply. Garrett pounded again and called, "Walter Sorenson! Open up!"

Inside the cabin, someone coughed and a gruff voice said, "Who is it?"

"My name is Garrett Yates. I'm here with Jamie's guardian. We need to talk to you."

Shuffling was followed by the thump of boots and the clang of the bolt being shot back. The door creaked and opened up a crack.

"What do you want with Jamie?" A man with a day's growth of whiskers and thinning, spiked hair seemed ready to slam the door in our faces, but Garrett rammed his boot into the opening.

"Jamie left a note. It said that he went with you for a ride, but his guardian," he indicated me with his hand, "Rachel McGivney, is worried sick. Is Jamie here with you?"

A sour expression distorted the man's features.

"We need to come in and talk about the boy," said Garrett.

Walter opened the door and stepped back. "All right, fine. Yeah, he's with us." He hitched his suspenders over his shoulders and unabashedly buttoned his pants.

I followed Garrett into the cabin and glanced around the room. It was the size of a big bedroom. To my left was a table, with a lantern casting flickering shadows. On the table were the remains of a fast-food meal, complete with three foil wrappers, spread open—one with a burger and chips that were hardly touched. An opened whiskey bottle and soda cans completed the charming picture, and were producing a stale smell that made me gag.

I glanced past the table to the wood-burning, pot-bellied stove, which crackled and cast a reddish glow. At least, it was warm in here.

"Where's Jamie?" I asked, fixing Walter with a steady gaze. I tried not to show my scorn for his actions, but my heart was pumping fast. I wanted to grab the man by the shirt collar and shake the truth out of him.

If I were six feet tall, I'd poke Walter in the nose, but at five foot four, I decided it was much smarter to keep my cool. I took a quick glance to the right, where a bunk bed was crammed into the corner. Some ridiculous part of me expected to see Jamie hiding under the covers of the top bunk, but the blanket was as flat as a board.

The lower bunk was wider, allowing room for two people. I bit my tongue and stifled any comment, as I noticed a naked woman with long red hair. Like a cat stretching, she pulled herself into a sitting position and gave Garrett a long sensuous look, while puckering her lips and slowly pulling the blankets to cover her breasts, leaving her bare shoulders showing

"Don't you have any decency, woman? Cover yourself." Walter snickered, picking up a robe from the floor and throwing it at the bed.

She reached for it and the blankets slipped again.

Feeling disgusted, I glowered at Garrett with a mixture of envy and jealousy over his obvious interest.

Walter guffawed.

I'd had enough. "Where is Jamie?" I demanded.

Walter seemed to find the sharpness in my voice comical. "You're a real little tiger cat." He raised his eyebrows at Garrett. "I bet you have fun with her."

I stared at the wall, my body rigid and forcing myself to regain my composure. "All we want to know is where Jamie is."

Walter ambled over to the stove, pulled an ember from the fire with a set of metal prongs, and took time lighting his cigarette. "What kids have to understand is they can't have their own way all the time. It's a question of give and take. You know what I mean?"

The pain in my stomach settled like a dead weight. What had I gotten Jamie into? I swallowed hard against my expanding panic.

Suddenly, Walter looked around the cabin as if he'd missed something. "Where's Elena? Why didn't she come for her kid herself?"

I tried not to blame him for his callous manner. "Surely you remember, Mr. Sorenson. Your wife died. I wrote it in the letter."

He gave an indifferent shrug. "She wasn't my wife. We parted ways a couple of years back."

A sense of helplessness filled me. I'd obviously written to a man who cared little for anyone, including his son.

"I've been busy lately, haven't I Delilah?" He eyed her.

I was sickened by his lack of concern over Jamie's safety. "He is your child—"

"No he isn't. Elena didn't want me having anything to do with him, so I let her keep him." Walter slapped his hands together in a gesture of indifference.

The sudden frenzy in my chest almost choked me.

"Why'd you take Jamie away?"

"You wrote the letter, lady. You didn't seem any too happy to have him."

The air crackled with the insensitivity of his words.

I stepped closer to Walter. "That is not true. All I wrote was that I thought Jamie should get to know his father. I thought you'd want to visit with your son."

Walter scowled. "You're wrong. The kid and I never did get along."

I wasn't ready to let Walter get away with such a lousy excuse for being so uncaring. "I saw a picture of you with Jamie. You'd been fishing. The two of you looked so happy."

Walter snorted. "A camera can lie. Elena always wanted me to stand beside the boy so she could pretend we were a happy family. Everything was a lie. She never could own up to the truth."

My lips quivered. "Don't speak that way about her. She was a good mom."

Walter rolled his eyes. "Listen lady, I've had enough of your high and mighty preaching. You can spare me the sermon. My ex-wife was no saint."

"We're not here to condemn anyone," said Garrett.

My temper flared. I wouldn't let Walter get away with smearing Elena's reputation. With a woman such as Delilah for company, I could only imagine his behavior. "When you were married, how many times did you cheat on Elena, and come home late with some feeble excuse?"

Walter shook his fist. "Don't go there, lady. You don't know what you're saying, so keep your mouth shut."

Garrett stepped between us. "Enough."

I backed off, shocked by the harshness in his voice.

Walter opened his mouth to say something, but apparently reconsidered, because he closed it and moved away.

"We came here to see Jamie. Where is he?" demanded Garrett.

"Ah, he's somewhere around." Walter waved his hand, indicating outside. "The little bugger didn't take well to Delilah, and created such a fuss that I told him to get out and not come back until he cooled off."

Anger surged in me. "Out there? He's a child and it's cold. How could you be so cruel?"

"He's a stubborn little hothead."

I raised my fist, but Garrett grabbed it before I could take a swing and poke Walter in the nose.

"How long has Jamie been outside?" Garrett asked.

Walter shrugged. "Don't rightly recall. Delilah and I have been busy." He picked up a soda can and chugged the contents. "The kid's probably hiding behind some tree, waiting for me to beg him to come back, but I'm not going to. Cooling off will do him some good."

"I doubt it," replied Garrett, his expression pensive. "Ms. McGivney and I will start a search for the boy in what little light we have left."

"Ah, don't worry. He'll come back. You can't trouble yourself every time they get their nose in a snit. Jamie's a smart kid. He won't freeze to death."

Garrett unzipped his jacket and pulled out his cell phone. "I'll call the police tonight and notify them of Jamie's location.

Walter shrugged. "No point in phoning. There's no cell service for miles around here. This is a dead zone."

Chapter Twenty-eight

Walter's words made my stomach constrict.

"We need your help, Mr. Sorenson," Garrett said, his tone making it very clear that there would be no debate. "There's very little daylight left. You, Rachel, and I can search the forest around the cabin."

I noticed Garrett hadn't included Delilah's name in the search and she obviously wasn't insulted. She wound her hair around her fingers, making long curls that rested on her shoulders.

"Do you have a flashlight?" asked Garrett.

Walter looked around the cabin. "Might be one in the cupboard." He went to a small nightstand beside the bed and winked at Delilah. "Be back really soon. Keep the bed warm."

He pinched Delilah's cheek, and she slapped his hand. "Cheeky bugger."

"Here it is." Walter held up a flashlight and clicked the switch.

I was relieved to see it was in working order. Now we could get on with our search.

Walter took his jacket and hat from a hook near the stove. For the first time, I sensed that he might be grasping the seriousness of Jamie's prolonged absence. His hat covered his forehead, shadowing his face and emphasizing his grim expression.

Outside, I shuffled along behind Garrett. Although it was only mid-afternoon, daylight was fading fast. The yellow sky glowed with an eerie beauty, outlining the rugged line of the snow-capped mountains. Although I'd lived all my life only a few hours away from the Rockies, I'd forgotten how impressive they were, and how cold and treacherous they could be.

Garrett put his arm around my shoulders, and steered me in the direction of the van, while he gave Walter instructions. "You take the area behind and to the right of the cabin. Rachel and I will work the area to the left. I'll get flashlights." While I waited beside the trunk of Walter's car, Garrett went into the van. I yanked my knit cap over my earlobes, pulled up my hood, and tied the cord under my chin. Then I rummaged in my pockets, took out a pair of fuzzy mittens, and pulled them over my leather gloves.

When Garrett stepped out of the van, I said, "Why don't we drive to the lodge and contact the police?"

"It would take too long on the winding road and the police wouldn't come till morning. They can't conduct a search at night."

What Garrett said was right, but my heart pounded faster at the thought of getting no help from law enforcement. The tension in my jaw made it ache. "We've got to find him tonight."

Garrett didn't answer. His serious expression scared me. He handed me a flashlight. "Here, you'll need this when we get into the trees."

A rush of gratitude for his support and cool-headed thinking filled me. I stuffed the flashlight into a deep pocket and followed him to the front of the van, where the plowed snow formed a five-foot ridge. Garrett scrambled up it first and I followed, anchoring one foot in the crusty snow and using my hands for balance as I climbed. I paused at the top of the bank. Below me, and to the right, stretched a huge meadow. The sun glinted on the snow, like sparkling diamonds, and under any other circumstances, I'd have enjoyed its beauty.

I got to the bottom of the ridge and discovered that the snow wasn't as deep as I had feared; hopefully walking would be easy.

"Look at these," Garrett yelled, the excitement in his voice encouraging me. "I've found Jamie's footprints."

I hurried toward him, sucking in cold air. Garrett directed his flashlight, revealing a line of prints. "Jamie came this way. He must have climbed the snowbank closer to the cabin somewhere."

Indentations showed where the snow had been disturbed, and my heart pounded faster as I pointed at the second set of tracks. "Scooter is with Jamie." I pressed my hand to my chest. "Thank goodness."

I closed my eyes. *Thank you.* New hope filled me. "We're going to find them tonight. It won't be long. I know Jamie and Scooter are going to be all right."

I looked at Garrett for reassurance, but all he said was, "I'm going to call for Walter. Jamie's tracks go across the meadow and disappear into the trees."

We didn't have to wait long for Walter. As we neared the edge of the clearing, he arrived, waving a flashlight in one hand and an ax in the other.

In his heavy parka and hood, and with his stubbly beard, he looked like a wild man. I shuddered to think I'd ever written to him.

Garrett's reaction was different. "Good, you brought an ax. Do you want to notch the trees?"

"Will do."

"Why are we wasting our time marking trees?" I asked. "Let's get going." I moved ahead of Garrett and trudged through the snow. Behind me, I could hear the men talking.

It was easy going so I picked up my speed. Garrett caught up with me and put his hand on my shoulder, forcing me to stop. "Slow down, Rachel. You have to pace yourself."

I shrugged his hand away. "I want this to be over. We have to find them tonight."

"You're going to follow behind me and stop berating yourself."

I pivoted and challenged him, anger spilling into my voice. "What's Walter doing?"

"He'll be behind us, notching the trees."

Without any more explanation, Garrett disappeared up the path and I hurried to catch up with him, attracted to his confident manner, and reassured by it.

Surrounded by forest on both sides, the trail was in good condition and easy to follow, but already dappled with shadows. At the sides, dead branches poked their dried, brown leaves through the snow. I called Jamie's name, paused for a few seconds, and then called twice more.

Garrett stopped walking and I did the same. I pushed my hood back and pulled my cap away from my ears, hoping to hear Jamie's voice. I rotated my shoulders in an effort to relieve the tension in them. The wind whispered through the trees and their tops swayed. I waited for a reply, but all I heard was the crunch of packed snow as Garrett resumed walking.

"Come on. We have to keep moving before it gets dark." The trees hushed his voice.

From behind me, Walter shouted Jamie's name, but there was no reply.

I trudged on for what seemed like hours, aiming the flashlight beam at Garrett's footprints, but the shadows darkened the ground, making the path harder to follow. Snowflakes fell softly on my face and melted against my skin. My muscles were shaking with exhaustion, but one question kept circling in my mind. How could Jamie stay outside all night?

I concentrated on every step I took. The path got steeper. Ahead of me Garrett stopped and yelled.

I shouted, hoping that our combined voices would reach Jamie. Walter joined our chorus and then, as if we were given a conductor's cue, we all stopped. The wind swished and the forest shapes merged into blackness.

I cocked my head and listened.

Nothing.

The silence was broken by Garrett. "We have to stop." He looked disgusted with the situation and terrified all at once. "Dammit! It's getting too dark. We have to go back to the cabin."

"Okay." Walter's quick reply shocked me. In a few seconds, Garrett was at my side.

"Why are we going back?" I demanded. "We can't leave Jamie up there! He'll freeze."

"It's too dark and dangerous, Rachel. We won't find him tonight."

"We can just stay on the path and keep yelling! We've got our flashlights. We can't stop!" I protested, although my inner voice told me to be reasonable and listen to Garrett. I was beating myself up. None of this would have happened if I hadn't sent the letter. It was all my fault.

"The batteries aren't going to last all night, and then where will we be? The three of us lost and frozen in the dark is not going to do Jamie any good." Garrett put his arm around my shoulder and coaxed me back along the path. "A storm is blowing in."

"It's only a little snow," I objected.

Garrett was quiet as we retraced our footsteps. Twigs snapped beneath our feet.

By the time we reached the meadow, snow was falling, making everything in front of us a blanket of white.

Garrett clutched my hand. "We don't want to get separated."

Walter walked beside us. The weather had changed. The wind howled and snow pellets bombarded my face. The cold prickled my nose. When we finally reached the banked snow near the cabin, Walter offered his hand to help me over and before I slapped it away, I caught myself. We were here to help Jamie and my personal dislike for Walter didn't matter. Warm light shone through the window and we stood on the porch, protected from the weather.

"You can stay the night." I was surprised at Walter's offer of hospitality. "There's a single bunk and pallets to sleep on."

I was glad Garrett declined. "We appreciate it, but I have thermal sleeping bags and we'll be fine in the van."

"Then we'll all be comfortable for the night," said Walter.

I must have looked horrified, because Walter added, "Jamie is dressed like a polar bear. The kid's clever. He's resilient and he's always had a survival sense."

I had to agree with him. Jamie was very clever. He had successfully hidden Scooter from me for months. It said a lot for his ingenuity and cleverness. I clung to the bit of hope Walter offered. I didn't know if he was praising Jamie to make me feel better or if he thought it was the truth. Either way, I gained a little respect for Walter.

We said goodnight, and Walter went into the cabin while Garrett and I stood on the porch. The cold and wind made me feel light-headed.

I swayed and Garrett put his arm around my waist. "There's nothing more we can do. Whatever happens tonight is up to Jamie."

Chapter Twenty-nine

I lifted my head, welcoming the snowflakes that numbed my skin and mingled with the tears on my cheeks.

"Come on, Rachel." Garrett held my elbow.

Our boots crunched through the hardened crust and the deep footprints were quickly filling with fresh snow. How would it be possible for Jamie to survive the night? Would he think to use leaves and make a bed for himself? Could he find dry ones? Maybe he could use boughs from trees for insulation.

I realized it was impossible.

Jamie didn't have an ax. How could he cut anything?

My hopes rested with the dog. If Scooter was with Jamie, they could snuggle together and Jamie would be kept warm. I remembered Garrett's comment about Scooter's thick fur and good health and it boosted my spirits. I'd read lots of stories where people had miraculously survived despite the elements, and I had to believe Jamie would be a survivor.

"Keep moving, Rachel." Garrett steered me toward the van. I pushed myself to keep putting one foot in front of the other until we reached the side doors. Garrett knocked the snow from his jacket and pants. I stood near him, flicking the snow from my knit cap and hood.

"There's not enough room for both of us to take off our wet boots at the same time. You go first and I'll wait out here until you've finished."

I stepped inside, took off my boots, and put my outer clothing on the back of a chair. Then I reached down and opened the door. "You can come in now."

Before he stepped up, I slipped into the sleeping area at the back. I sat on the left bed, worrying about Jamie.

Once Garrett finished taking off his outer clothing, he said, "It's freezing in here. I'll get the furnace going for a little while."

I heard the whirring of a fan, followed by three clicks and Garrett explained, "That's the igniter lighting the furnace. In a moment or two, there'll be warm air from the vent by your feet."

I let my feet dangle over the edge of the bed while I leaned forward to watch Garrett in the kitchen. He opened the cupboard behind the driver's seat and got two bottles of water. He held them up. "In the winter, there's antifreeze in the lines and I have to dry camp, so I always carry an extra supply of water with me."

He emptied the water into a saucepan. "I have to use the propane stove, since I can't plug in the kettle." He struck a match and held it to the burner.

It whooshed.

My legs and feet were getting warm from the heat blowing on my ankles and I thought of one little boy who'd be very cold.

"Drink some tea. I promise it'll make you feel better."

Garrett handed me a steaming mug and I put it on the table between the two beds. I didn't look at him when he sat across from me on the other bed. Under different circumstances, I might have enjoyed the intimacy, but I was here because of my mistake and Garrett's silence masked a hundred condemnations. The longer we sat, the more I could feel a tremendous pressure pushing on my shoulders, reminding me of all my guilt—past and present.

After several minutes, he moved and sat beside me. He put his hand under my chin, tilting it up so I had to look him in the eye, and asked me softly, "Why did you write the letter to Walter?"

I didn't tell him that it was because of a dozen incidents. In hindsight, they all sounded trivial. Dug up tulips, poop on the rug, upturned flowerpots, and most of importantly—or so it had seemed—a child who really didn't want me for his guardian, and who had let me know it with three simple words. It was as if a dagger were plunged into my chest ... and in my anger and hurt, I'd struck back by mailing the letter.

"I didn't want him," I whispered.

Garrett sucked a breath in. "Why?"

"Jamie said he hated me, and I believed him." My words sounded hardhearted, but it was the truth. At first I *hadn't* wanted Jamie, but now I couldn't bear the thought of *not* having him. My life would be orderly, and regulated, but boring without the overwhelming caring and affection I experienced every time he came home from school or even from riding his bike.

Doubt crashed in on me, and I blamed Garrett. "I was afraid something like this might happen. I told you and Elena that I wasn't going to be a good guardian."

Garrett let his hands drop. I pulled back and put my feet up on the bed, hugging my knees to my chest and making more space between us.

"Do you really trust yourself so little?" His gaze held me, and the huge hollowness in my chest threatened to collapse, plunging me into a pit of darkness.

He took my hand and caressed it as he spoke, sending shivers through me. "I remember you, back in our teens, being an honest, hardworking girl. You were quieter and more mature than the rest of us. When Don asked if I'd help him at his firm, I found out that you were in Maryville again, not married, and didn't have a child and it struck me that you'd be a good mother."

"So you decided for me? *You* pressured Elena to pick me? What right did you have to interfere with my life?" I shuddered at the implication of my own words, that Jamie had been nothing more to me than an interruption, but it was true—at first. Jamie *did* interfere, but slowly my feelings had changed. Unfortunately, by that time, I'd already made the mistake and mailed the letter. I glanced away from Garrett's questioning gaze.

He cradled my hand in his, sharing the warmth. "My faith in you was strong."

I noticed that he used the past tense. Everything had changed.

"Faith in me? Well, you were wrong to have it." I tried to keep my lips from shaking and my voice from cracking, but he had to know the truth.

"I was afraid to take Jamie because ... because I've already killed one little boy."

Chapter Thirty

Garrett let my hand go. His lower lip dropped and his upper lip curled in disbelief and horror. His mouth moved, but no words came out. He stared at me and blinked, as if he were seeing some monster for the first time, but couldn't comprehend what he saw. "You couldn't kill a child. I don't believe you."

I raised my chin and answered sharply. "It's the truth, whether you believe it or not."

"What do you mean, Rachel? You haven't killed anyone. You *couldn't* harm anyone. I don't believe it. Not you." His words sounded encouraging, but an edge of doubt sharpened his tone.

I backed into the corner of the bed. The walls were cold on my back. "How well do you know me? You think you know everything. You don't." I wanted to shock him, to make him realize that taking Jamie had been a mistake from the beginning. I wanted to lay the responsibility on his shoulders, not on mine where it belonged.

He frowned, my answer catching him unawares. He moved closer still and put his hands on my shoulders.

"Tell me everything."

I bowed my head and pressed my hands together. "When I was seven, I killed my three-year-old brother and it's haunted me for years. I shouldn't have taken Jamie, but you forced me." I wanted the words to hurt him and make him realize that he was partly to blame for this ordeal. "If you hadn't pushed Elena to accept me as Jamie's guardian, none of this would have happened. I didn't want Jamie. I *knew* he wouldn't be safe with me."

Without a word, Garrett moved across the narrow space and back to his own bed. He rested his head in his hands and I slumped into the corner. My words had finally registered and his silence exposed his contempt. It hung in the air like an invisible force and a chasm of distrust and misunderstanding opened between us.

I crossed my arms over my chest and closed my eyes. I had never wanted to look back at the bits and pieces I remembered of that fatal day, but the nightmare lingered and the overwhelming ache never went away.

"What happened?"

I wiped the tears from my face and clutched the corner of the sheet. I cleared my throat. "Andy was a baby—an innocent soul—and after his death there was an unspoken rule between my mother and me that we would never discuss him. We didn't have any happy family photos or pictures in our trailer. It was as if he'd never existed."

I faltered. I'd chosen to bury my memories of Andy in a dark corner of my mind, shutting away the sorrow, but Jamie's disappearance had blasted the door open and snippets of memories were seeping out.

"Go on."

Garrett's words were soothing and I continued, "During my childhood and teens, I never saw any pictures of Andy. After my mother died, I found a box of old photos hidden in in her bedroom along with her personal belongings. They brought back both sad and happy memories. I remembered Andy's chubby cheeks and how he used to call me Ray." The words choked my throat. "He never quite learned to say Rachel," I explained.

"He'd wait for me at the gate in the front yard, and

when I came home from school, he'd say 'Ray, Ray' and hold up his little arms. I'd drop my school books in the house, take his hand, and we'd walk outside around the pool. In winter it was covered, but in summer we could go swimming anytime, as long as I never left Andy alone."

I swallowed hard, fighting the surge of desperation that came with knowing I might never see Jamie alive again, just like Andy.

Sensing that I was getting overwhelmed, Garrett leaned over and put a comforting hand on my arm. "It's okay, Rachel. I'm going to make us another cup of tea, and then you can continue. All right?" I nodded, and he got two bottles of water, emptying them into the saucepan. Then I heard the now familiar whoosh as he turned the burner knob.

I sat on the edge of the bed, staring across to the opposite window. The blind hadn't been closed and I saw my grief-stricken reflection.

After a few minutes, Garrett handed me a mug. "Here you go. It'll warm your hands and make you feel better."

"Thanks." I reached for the mug, wrapping my fingers around it and letting the warmth seep into my hands. I had one sip. Then I placed the mug on the table, toying with the tea bag's string, dunking the bag repeatedly and watching as the water darkened. Andy's small face seemed to blend with Jamie's in my mind. Both were filled with fear.

Garrett ducked as he stepped back into the bedroom. He placed his mug next to mine and sat on his bed.

I avoided his gaze and concentrated on cooling my tea by blowing across the surface.

"Let's hear the rest."

My hands shaking, I put the mug down, trying to focus on the distant loss of my brother, and suppress the near panic that arose when I thought of what could be happening to Jamie in that very moment.

I closed my eyes, taking a few deep breaths and trying to put myself back into that time and place, because I knew that almost any place would be better than where I found myself at present. "I remember coming home from school. I had a headache, but Andy wanted to go swimming and I didn't want to disappoint him. He'd waited for me all day. I took him to the pool, and soon after, my mom came into the backyard with a flat of geraniums to be planted. Our backyard was surrounded by a high, cement wall. Between the pool deck and the fence was a three-foot-wide flowerbed. My mom was busy planting the bright red flowers she loved, and her back was to Andy and me. Andy had water wings on his little arms and we splashed each other. He giggled." I smiled for a moment, remembering Andy's grin and his baby face.

"Go on with your story."

I took a sip of tea before I continued. "I told my mom I had a headache and wanted to go to bed. She said I had to stay with Andy. She needed to get the flowers planted, but I didn't listen to her. My stomach felt queasy and I thought I was going to puke, so I climbed out of the pool, went to the bathroom, and was sick to my stomach. Afterward, I crashed on my bed and fell asleep. I'd forgotten Andy."

I sniffed and wiped my nose with a tissue Garrett handed me. I took another sip of tea—the warm liquid soothing my throat.

"The next thing I remember, I woke up to my mother yelling. I jumped out of bed and ran outside. Andy was lying on the pool deck with my mom over him, breathing into his mouth. My stepdad was on the telephone, and after he hung up, he shouted to my mom that the ambulance was coming. It seemed a long time before I could hear sirens blaring.

"My mom screamed when they told her that it was too late. Andy was dead. His little body was so small on that gurney."

I stopped. The tears were streaming down my cheeks and I bowed my head, absorbed with my guilt. In my mind, I could see Andy now, as clearly as if I were standing at his side. "The paramedics put Andy in the ambulance and I never saw him again," I murmured, struggling against the thickness in my throat. Garrett's face was masked in shadow and I took his silence as an indication that he wanted me to continue.

I brushed my eyes with the back of my hand. "Andy was dead … and it was my fault because I'd left him alone in the pool. After his death, my mom and dad hardly talked to each. When they weren't ignoring each other, they were screaming. Andy was my stepfather's and mother's child. Both my parents hated me because I'd killed their darling little boy." I gulped, my body shaking.

Garrett sat beside me and put his arm around my shoulder, drawing me to his side. "You're not to blame."

His warm hug and consoling words were meant to comfort me, but I couldn't believe him.

"I remember hearing my mother telling my stepdad that she'd be happy if she never saw him again. He told her, 'That can be arranged.' He left a few days later and I never saw or heard from him again."

"Your parents' words," said Garrett, "were spoken out of grief." He shifted to his bed, and sat on the edge, watching me.

I stared at the floor, wanting to ask a question that had haunted me for years. *Why didn't my stepdad ever come back to see me … or at least write? My biological father had left my mother when he found out she was pregnant.* I didn't know if either man was dead or alive. All I knew was that I wanted to be with my stepdad and have his love. I had thought that Jamie needed the same attention, but I'd been wrong. Walter didn't love Jamie … any more than my stepfather had loved me.

I raised my head and gazed at Garrett. "When Jamie

said he hated me, I had to do something. I believed that he'd be happier with his father … so I mailed the letter."

"Why didn't you come and talk to me first?"

His question surprised me. "Would it have made any difference? I don't think we've ever *really* talked."

He frowned. "What? We've talked plenty of times." He sounded confused and hurt. "We've discussed Jamie. I've visited you. I've eaten supper with you. We went to Jamie's concert together. I've showed you my van! I have believed in you all these years …. even when you haven't believed in yourself! What more do you want?"

I exhaled. All of that was true. "But you've never once told me if you even *like* me."

His eyebrows shot up. "I've been helping you at every opportunity. Haven't you figured it out?"

I knew Garrett was a man of few words, but I didn't realize that—to him—showing someone your van was the height of intimacy

He sighed and got back to his original point. "You could have come to me, Rachel. I would have understood. Just like I understand that your brother's death wasn't your fault."

His statement should have reassured me, but my shoulders slumped and I twisted the edge of the pillow case, unable to meet his probing gaze. "My mother told me what to do and I disobeyed."

"And so you've been punishing yourself ever since."

"I deserve to be punished. I let my brother die. It wouldn't have happened if I hadn't left him. He'd still be alive"

Garrett sat on my right side, and draped his arm over my shoulder. His fingers brushed my neck and he cupped my chin with his hand, gently turning my head so that I was looking at him. "You were a child," he said.

I couldn't keep the pain out of my voice. "My little

brother died and I can never bring him back."

"There was an adult present. *You* were only seven years old. You couldn't be entirely responsible for a little boy." His voice poured over me like warm, soothing oil.

"But I let my mom down." My voice quivered. "I miss Andy. I wonder what he'd be like—all grown up. Would he be married? What kind of work would he do? Would he have a family?" A tear rolled down my cheek. Garrett wiped it away.

"You can't change the past." He kissed my forehead and brushed his mouth against my temple. "All we have is right now and we're doing the best we can." His mouth grazed my cheek, and I leaned my head against his chest. His breath warmed my ear, tickled it, and I trembled.

I was surrounded by darkness and cold, by memories I didn't want to relive, and a present so terrifying that I couldn't bear to think about it. I couldn't *let* myself think about anything that was happening outside of the safety and comfort of Garrett's arms, so I pressed against him—a feverish warmth coiling through me. I wanted to forget everything. I wanted to still the torment that plagued me. All I wanted was now. "Make love to me," I whispered.

Chapter Thirty-one

He jerked as if I'd poured scalding water over him, and held me at arm's length, squinting at me in the dim light: "You don't know what you're saying."

When I didn't answer, he gave me a gentle shake. "You're worried about Jamie and you're vulnerable. I won't have you doing something tonight that you might regret tomorrow." He leaned closer, seeming to sense the feeling of rejection that was growing in me, and wanting to stop it before it took root. "Over the years, I've never forgotten you ... and I've always wondered what it'd be like to make love to you. But as much as you tempt me, tonight is not the right time."

He got to his feet and slipped to the front of the van. "You'd better get some sleep. It's going to be an early morning."

I wanted him to come back, but he opened the bi-fold bathroom door, blocking my view. I heard him rifling around in the closet, and after a long moment, he peered around the door. "Get undressed," he instructed.

I blinked, and my mouth dropped open. "What?" I didn't understand his sudden change of heart.

He handed me a pile of clothes. "These pajamas and socks will keep you warm in the sleeping bag."

I caught a glint of amusement in his eyes. "Don't worry. I haven't changed my mind. I'm not going to *ravish you*, if that's what you're thinking." He seemed to be mocking the language from some frivolous romance novel.

I straightened up, but couldn't stand tall without my head bumping the ceiling. "Of course you wouldn't. You're a gentleman." I reflected back on our ridiculously slow courtship.

"Clearly, you've never really been inside a man's head. Put these on." He indicated the flannel pajamas. "They're freshly laundered, but you'll have to roll them up at the waist. The sleeping bag is Arctic quality. Trust me, you'll be comfortable."

I nodded, all the time wondering how I was going to change without being in full view of Garrett. Once again, he seemed to read my mind and a slow smile crossed his face. "You don't need to worry. You'll have your privacy. If it makes you happy though, I'll sit in the captain's chair and promise to keep my eyes straight ahead."

I stood up while he opened the bathroom door and disappeared from sight. Paper rustled. I took off my outer clothing and stood for a moment in my bra and panties, realizing that I'd be more comfortable without underwear. I hesitated to totally strip, though.

I peeked around the bi-fold. Garrett had been true to his word—about not peeking at least. He was too busy undressing to do so. He had his back to me. His belt buckle jingled as his pants dropped to the floor. He leaned over to pick them up and I stared at his muscular legs and the black undershorts hugging his butt.

My stomach tightened and I stepped back. The floor creaked.

"You okay?" asked Garrett.

"I'm fine, perfectly fine," I replied, as I stripped off my underwear and got into his pajamas. I rolled up the sleeves and folded the material at the waist.

"Are you decent? Can I come back?"

"Certainly." I'd tried to sound confident.

Why had I been so stupid as to ask him to make love to me? I didn't ask him, I begged. Not in so many words, but I'd heard the pleading in my tone and I wanted to forget the vow I'd made to my mother over two decades ago that I wouldn't sleep with a man until we married.

In a single moment of madness I'd been ready to make love to this man. No, it wouldn't have been love. It'd have been for my own satisfaction to quell the despair and desire burning inside—a way to purge my soul of the heartbreak and hunger.

The only way I could rationalize it was that I'd made the comment out of desperation and guilt over what I'd done. I'd neglected my duty twice and this time there could be the same tragic consequence as there'd been with my brother. In a moment of desperation, I wanted to forget and have Garrett wipe the horrible memories from my mind. For a few minutes I wanted to be worry free. I carried on with getting ready for bed, determined not to make a fool of myself again.

I was busy unzipping the sleeping bag cover when Garrett backed cautiously into the bedroom. I tried not to notice the white t-shirt hugging the muscles of his back, and his tight black shorts.

Shocked with myself for ogling, I glanced away, but not before I sneaked one last approving look.

He turned and eyed me with a confident smile. "I was gentlemanly enough not to peek at you; I had assumed you were a lady and would afford me the same courtesy."

I knew he was teasing me, but I was still embarrassed that I'd been caught. I tried to defend my actions. "I was going to open the bi-fold to let you know I was ready."

"But instead you decided to watch the show. I hope you enjoyed it," he taunted with a provocative grin.

"I …" I began, but didn't know how to defend my

actions. "I'm sorry if I offended you."

He raised his eyebrow. "Who said I found it offensive?"

"No, but ..."

He saved me further embarrassment when he got busy unrolling his sleeping bag and straightening it on the bed. Kneeling down, I punched the pillow he'd given me and placed it at the head of the bed. Out of the corner of my eye, I saw Garrett stop working and look at me. I gave the pillow a few extra punches, and then sat on the bed with my knees tucked close to my chest as I pulled on the socks. I removed the bobby pins from my hair and shook my head. My hair swished over my shoulders and I combed it with my hands, enjoying the feeling of freedom before I tucked one side behind my ear.

Garrett stood with one forearm resting against the ceiling above him, watching me. He ducked his head, leaned toward me, and took my hand, preventing me from twisting my hair into a braid.

"Let it fall naturally, over your shoulders. It's soft and I like it."

A devastating smile lifted the corners of his mouth and he stroked my cheek, sending shivers down my spine. "Your hair reminds me of a beautiful, young girl I once knew." He slid his fingers over my chin and I trembled at his touch. A tide of longing rippled all the way through me and down the back of my legs.

He rested his open hand against the side of my face and I turned my head so that my lips touched his palm.

He let out a sigh. "I've always respected you, Rachel, since you were seventeen years old. You should know by now that I haven't changed my mind about that." He pulled his hand away and sat on the bed facing me, his mouth set in a hard line.

My stomach gave a funny little lurch. "I do know," I protested.

"Don't be ashamed of what you said before." Garrett said softly, and frowned, as if an idea just occurred to him. "You're not afraid of me, are you? Worried I'll take you up on your offer?"

I blushed and swallowed, already regretting my bold words. "I've never been ..." I couldn't tell him.

"What?" he asked gently. "What have you never been? You explained about your brother. What else do you think you've done wrong?"

I bit my bottom lip. "It's not exactly wrong. It's ... well, you see, I don't quite know how to tell you this, but ... you already know that in high school I didn't have any dates."

Garrett gave an indifferent shrug. "High school dating is overrated."

I wouldn't tell him about my lonely teen years, so I chose to explain about later, about what I'd done after high school. "I left Maryville and went to university. Mom had managed to save some money for my tuition and she had a small insurance policy, but I had to work while I was in school in order to have enough money to cover living expenses. And so I never really got around to ..." I rubbed my sweaty palm against my legs.

Deflecting the conversation from my lack of experience, I took the offensive. "I don't suppose you ever had to worry about running out of money by the end of the month."

"You know so very little about me. Don't assume you know what I did or didn't have."

For several minutes, I was at a loss for words. Did I want to divulge my secret? What would he say?

"Whatever is bothering you, just say it. It will be okay."

I avoided his gaze, somehow knowing that he spoke the truth. I took a fortifying breath. "I'm a thirty-eight-year-old virgin," I blurted out. My lower lip quivered.

He was surprised, to say the least. "Oh," he said softly,

and then he was the one to avoid eye contact. "Well, I suppose, thinking back to some of our earlier conversations, that doesn't come entirely out of left field," he murmured, almost to himself. He looked at me without expression, and his scrutiny made me squirm. He held my forearm and stepped into the kitchen, pulling me along with him. Then he spun me around, and stared straight at me.

"Didn't you know that I've always been concerned about you, and wanted the best for you? I knew you'd moved back to Maryville." His gaze lowered and lingered on my mouth. "I've thought about you many times and wondered what it'd be like to hold you and kiss you."

I licked away the dryness on my lower lip.

"Don't do that."

I hesitated, and then laughed. "Why?" I asked, grinning up at him. "My lips are dry."

I felt tight inside, over-wound and surprisingly daring.

Our eyes caught and held.

He drew me close. I wrapped my arms around his back, closed my eyes, and tilted my head. His lips brushed mine. He flattened his hand against my back and pressed me nearer, until I felt his heart thumping and his ragged breath.

His lips covered mine, drawing me even closer and enclosing me in his warmth. I molded my body to his. As quickly as the kiss began, it stopped. Garrett held me at arm's length, his face registering conviction, and regret. Then he pulled me closer and for a long moment, we just held each other, thinking about where we found ourselves. We thought about the young boy who had brought us back together, and whose absence threatened to tear us both apart. I knew that Garrett cared about Jamie almost as much as I did, and wondered if he was struggling as hard as I was not to think about what was happening out there in the cold and snow— out there beyond our reach, beyond our control.

Finally, he leaned back and caressed my cheek, letting out a slow, shaking breath. "This is *not* the right time." His voice was persuasive, and I could almost see him shoring up his resolve to be strong for us both. "But when it is, you'd better watch out."

He twisted me around so I faced the back of the van. "Go to bed and don't tempt me anymore." He nudged me forward.

Without saying another word, I stepped into the bedroom and crawled into my sleeping bag. I pulled the cover around my shoulders, and snuggled into the pillow.

When I was settled, Garrett said, "Goodnight, Rachel. Tomorrow we'll bring Jamie home."

Like liquid honey, his words were soothing in the darkness and they sent a surge of hope through me. In a few minutes, his even breathing assured me that he was asleep. I was getting warm and cozy, cocooned in the semidarkness, but I couldn't relax. Not when Jamie was in such danger ... and not when I had just been so willing to make love to Garrett. A thousand feelings were wrestling for control of my consciousness, and it seemed like all of them were terrifying in one way or another. Silently, I thanked Garrett for being so strong, and stopping me. He was right. It wasn't the right time.

We were there for something far more important—Jamie. Where was he? What was he doing? I could only hope Garrett was right and that somehow Jamie would survive this night. Tomorrow we'd bring him home.

Chapter Thirty-two

As I lay in the sleeping bag, trying not to give in to the tears that threatened to escape whenever I thought of Jamie, out there on the mountain all alone, memories of a different anguish, which I'd always suppressed, flashed through my mind. After Andy's drowning, my thoughts of him moved into a twilight zone and my mother never said his name. With my brother dead and my stepfather gone, I believed that Mom had lost what was most precious to her. I'd wanted her to hug me and tell me that she loved me, but all she did was work. At the time, I never realized how she needed to keep a roof over our heads and food on the table. By my teenage years, I'd grown indifferent to her. At night she'd come home late from the diner, too tired to talk and when she did it was a lecture about not letting a man have his way with me.

I hadn't made life easier for her. I'd balked at her suggestion of me working in the diner. I didn't mind hard work, but I was ashamed of my mother and her boisterous manner with customers. She'd put on a smile and joke with them. Failing to realize that it was just part of the job, I was jealous of her apparent interest in them, when she lacked any interest whatsoever in me. At home, she'd flop onto the sofa, massage her temples, and ask me what I learned in school. I'd reply, "Nothing."

She was doing her very best for me. In return, I'd

condemned her over and over. Why didn't she take me shopping? Why wasn't she happy and funny with me? A thousand criticisms filled my mind and I would remember the perfect life our family had enjoyed before my brother died.

It wasn't true. Our life hadn't been perfect. My parents argued and yelled at each other, and I would hide under the crib, cuddling Andy and humming to drown out the noise. Once the fights stopped, I would hug my brother and kiss away his tears. As soon as my mom came into my bedroom to say goodnight, I'd pretend I was asleep, and wouldn't speak when she kissed me on the forehead.

After my parents' breakup, I was ashamed of where mom and I lived, and never invited anyone over. The mobile home residents were called trailer trash and I never forgot it. I realized I'd grown from a fearful kid into an anxious adult, and when Scooter made a mess on my beautiful silk rug, all the disgusting memories of the mobile home carpet came flooding back. I couldn't change my childhood. It was what it was and there was no going back. But I could change.

I promised myself that, if I was so lucky as to get a second chance with Jamie, I'd be less concerned about the picky little things in life.

All that really mattered was caring for Jamie and telling him that I loved him.

Chapter Thirty-three

The first light of dawn was appearing over the mountain when Garrett called from the kitchen to wake me. "Rachel, it's time to get up. I'm making coffee."

I rolled over in the cramped bed and unwound the sheets. The other bed was made and the pillow tucked under the bedspread. My pants, t-shirt, and sweater were folded in a pile and placed on Garrett's bed. I heard a spoon clink against a coffee cup. He stepped between the two beds, and placed a mug and a plate with a bagel on the table. He tilted his head and looked at me. "I'll eat up front so you can get dressed."

"Thanks." I waited until he'd retreated to the kitchen and opened the bi-fold.

I stripped off the pajamas, took my bra and panties from under my pillow, and got into my clothes.

"As soon as you're ready, we'll start out. I'm going to the cabin for a minute. I'll be right back."

He stepped outside. Between bites of the bagel, I sipped at the coffee, but with my anxiety over Jamie, I couldn't eat much. I was placing the dishes in the sink when Garrett came back and I told him that I was ready to go.

"Good. I woke the two love birds." A glint of satisfaction flared in his eyes. "Walter and Delilah are taking the car and contacting the police once they're out of this dead zone." His momentary pleasure was replaced by bleakness.

"Do you think there's a chance for Jamie?" I asked.

"There's always a chance." He leaned over and gave me a kiss on the forehead, reassuring me as though I were a child whose nightmare needed to be chased away by a kindly parent.

He helped me into my jacket. In silence, we both put on our knit caps, boots, and mittens. Garrett went out first and I followed. The icy air nipped my exposed skin. Ordinarily I would have loved the freshness of the mountains, but this morning fear gnawed at me, along with the burning question: Did Jamie make it through the night?

Walter wasn't outside, so we went to the cabin and Garrett pounded on the door. "Walter, it's time to get going."

Walter emerged, wearing snow boots, a heavy parka, and a furry hat. Delilah followed in a long, white fur coat, which I guessed was mink. She had a matching hat, something I imagined a Cossack might wear. Her long, red hair curled down to her shoulders, reminding me of an aging movie star. Was that what had charmed Walter?

I shook my head, thinking I was naive. Obviously it had been Delilah's other attributes that had enticed him. She held a cigarette between her fingers, and the brightly painted nails on her pale, white hands made me think of blotches of blood on snow.

"I didn't want to come here," she whined and puffed at her smoke.

Walter stomped toward the car. "Bull. You said you wanted to go to the mountains and have time alone with me. Well, you got both." He gave her a shameless leer.

"Ugh." Delilah reared her head back like a high-strung mare. "In this dump, with an outhouse? Who are you kidding? I thought you had a country estate."

"Yeah, sure. Just like I've got a brand new Lamborghini over there." He pointed to his midsized car.

Delilah pouted and Walter held his hand out, pressing the car fob. The locks clicked open. Garrett stepped forward to hold Delilah's arm and she clung to him, tottering in her high-heeled boots as he opened the passenger door.

Before she got in the car, Delilah put her hand on Garrett's shoulder, giving him an air kiss. "You know how to treat a girl. You, sir, are a true gentleman. How can I ever thank you?"

Her purring made me want to scream.

I didn't have to say anything. Garrett put his hand on Delilah's arm, his voice low and serious. "By contacting the police and letting them know about Jamie." He closed the door and gave Delilah an impersonal smile.

The car slowly pulled away and I was thankful that Walter apparently had the brains to drive carefully.

I knew that whatever happened in the next few hours would affect me for the rest of my life.

Chapter Thirty-four

Once Walter's car disappeared, Garrett turned to me. "Are you ready?"

I nodded. It was still sunny, but as I glanced upwards, the weather didn't seem promising. Snow fell softly. After we climbed the drift and moved into the clearing, I searched for Jamie and Scooter's footprints, but they'd been lost in last night's whiteout.

Stretching before us was the pristine meadow, and beyond it, the dark forest.

I kept pace with Garrett, anxious to reach the trees. "We'll find Jamie. It'll all work out."

I didn't know where he'd found this new optimism, and I didn't bother asking.

If Jamie and I were at home, he'd be outside playing with Scooter in the backyard or in the field at the end of the block. When he came inside, I'd make him hot milk with chocolate. There were so many things I wanted to do with Jamie, and I promised myself that—if I got the chance—I would take the time to enjoy every moment with him.

We plodded along and in some places the snow was deeper, covering my boots up to the ankles.

Finally we reached the forest. The snow had drifted into mounds around the bushes and trees. The path we'd followed last night was a maze of entwined shapes, brightness and shadows, but no footprints.

"We can't see the path. How are we going to find Jamie?"

Garrett grinned, and a flicker of anger pumped through me. How could he smile with Jamie still missing?

He pointed to a notch above my head. "Remember? Walter marked the trees."

I saw the fresh cut mark. Walter had done something right. Garrett plowed through the snow and pointed to another notch.

A new surge of energy filled me and I tromped up the path, ahead of Garrett and keeping a sharp lookout for more notched trees. Every new one filled me with revived hope. "We're going to find Jamie."

I didn't wait for Garrett's answer before shouting, "Jamie!" I repeated it three more times, but there was no answer. My new-found hope withered.

After climbing for half an hour, I couldn't see any more notches on the trees, I hesitated. In all directions, the trees seemed to blend and blur into patterns of light and shadow. I didn't have a clue which way to go. My hands and face tingled.

"I'll lead from here." Garrett was behind me and I stopped, giving him room to get ahead. The route was getting steeper and the drifts deeper. I cautiously followed, stepping into Garrett's tracks, but the drifts disguised uneven ground. I stumbled and clutched at tree trunks to keep my balance.

"Jamie!" I yelled. "Jamie."

"Be quiet, Rachel." Garrett's sharp order caught me by surprise and I stopped.

Branches snapped, and I heard a dog barking. It got louder and I had a fluttery feeling in my stomach. Was that Scooter? And was he with Jamie?

The dog bounded out of the trees and jumped at me, knocking me backwards. I landed in a pile of snow, with

Scooter licking my cheeks and drool splashing my chin. I tried to wipe it away.

"Where's Jamie?" I asked, as if the dog would understand. Before I could grab his collar, Scooter took off, disappearing up the mountain. "Come back," I yelled, realizing that he'd never obeyed me before, but if Scooter was here, surely Jamie had to be close by. A wave of anxiety hit me in the chest.

Garrett offered me a hand and I got to my feet, my only concern being that we might lose Scooter. We didn't need to worry. Scooter kept up a continuous chorus of barks. I hurried past Garrett and we followed the dog. Flashes of dark gray and white fur flickered between the trees, as if some forest spirit guided our way. We scrambled over rocks, the climb getting more difficult. I gasped for breath.

Just when I thought we'd never find him, I heard Jamie's voice calling my name. "Rachel!"

I paused, holding my breath and straining to hear. There it was again. "Rachel!" He sounded closer.

Then, between the trees, I saw a flash of red from his jacket, as he ran toward us with his hood flapping. He reminded me of a squirrel scrambling over the snow in winter.

As Jamie got nearer, I put my arms out and he hugged me around the waist. I leaned over and pulled him closer, wrapping him in my warmth. His hood was freezing cold against my nose as our cheeks rubbed together. Tears spilled and I wasn't sure whether they were mine or his.

"You're safe," I murmured and kissed his cheek.

"Yes." He shivered. "You're not as warm as Scooter."

The dog danced around and jumped against us. I didn't care. All I wanted was Jamie and I held him, savoring the moment, and knowing that everything had changed. From now on, I'd cherish each day with the little boy I'd come to love.

Chapter Thirty-five

One week later, Jamie and I sat at the kitchen table eating breakfast. He stuffed cereal into his mouth, looked up, and grinned at me while a dribble of milk spilled down his chin. I quashed the urge to correct him on his manners. What was a little spilled milk when Jamie was healthy and happy?

Since we'd found him, I'd had to stop myself from hovering. He was an independent little boy who had survived a night in the mountains. Of course, a lot of credit for that went to Scooter.

I glanced at the entrance to the kitchen. Scooter lay with his paws stretched out in front of him and his head resting on them. As soon as he knew I was looking at him, he whined and got to his feet, with his tail wagging.

"Okay, come on over here." I slapped my leg and Scooter padded to the table and sat beside me, begging for something to eat.

I had to admit, I was rather pleased with his show of obedience and affection. I didn't know whether he was really clever, or just smart enough to realize a good thing when he saw it. I was his meal ticket, but I didn't believe in feeding him table scraps.

Scooter gave one more little whine.

"He likes you, Rachel." Jamie's face glowed.

Both Jamie and Scooter were making my defenses

crumble. I stared at the dog, trying not to encourage him. "Don't think those big eyes are going to make me change my mind. You are not getting anything to eat."

I could have sworn Scooter understood everything I said. He moved closer to Jamie.

"You're a good boy." Jamie rubbed the top of the dog's head. Scooter had a dreamy look in his eyes, as if he'd won the doggy-bone lottery jackpot.

I agreed with him. Every time I looked at Jamie, I wanted to hug him and never let him out of my sight, but I was determined I wouldn't become a helicopter parent.

I still marveled at his ingenuity, the way he could think on his feet. He'd kept Scooter hidden from me for months. I wasn't sure if it showed that Jamie was really clever or I was really stupid, but I hoped it was the former.

"So tell me again how you found the hut?"

Jamie didn't seem to mind repeating his story. "I was really mad at Walter. Delilah's so dumb; I wanted to get away from her." He stroked Scooter. "Besides, she didn't like my dog."

His comment cut close to home. "I didn't like Scooter at first, either. Remember I wanted you to get rid of him?"

"You've changed."

Trust a kid to see the truth and give a dead-on comment. I wasn't sure I deserved his open approval, but I had to admit that Scooter had gone from unwelcome mutt to hero dog.

"Delilah's got nails like this." Jamie put his hands in front of his face and wiggled his fingers. "Maybe she's an evil witch from the forest."

I agreed. Delilah's long nails had reminded me of blood, but I didn't need to give Jamie any more ideas. I remained silent and he continued.

"Scooter and I ran to the forest and up the path. We never stopped until we came to the hut. We went inside to look around. I was mad at my dad, and it was cold and starting to snow."

My heart clenched and I pressed my hand against my chest, reliving the fear. "I didn't know how you'd survive the night. I was so worried."

Jamie's face puckered. "I'm not a baby. I found a box of matches on a shelf and I lighted a fire."

His chest seemed to expand and it felt like the backs of my eyes were watering. I wanted to laugh with relief at his words, and at the same time, cry at what I could have lost. I'd come to believe Jamie was an old soul. It was as if he understood things adults didn't, or at least not *this* adult. He had challenged my beliefs.

"Tell me again about the fire."

"It was easy. I'd watched Walter start one with the kindling. He let the fire grow before he put a larger piece in the stove." A mischievous grin crossed his face. "Delilah screamed about the cold, the smell, the food, and the outhouse."

I realized Jamie had started to call his dad by his first name and I hadn't corrected him. I figured it was Jamie's choice. The adventure had changed his attitude toward Walter. Part of me was sad that Jamie didn't feel a link to his own father anymore, but I wasn't sure the man deserved a son like Jamie.

"Delilah's a weird name and she's horrible." Jamie opened his mouth, stuck out his tongue, and pointed into his mouth with his index finger, making a gagging sound.

I thought Delilah's name fit her perfectly. I could imagine her with Samson, enjoying decadent pleasures, while plotting to destroy him.

"Every time Delilah had to use the outhouse, she screamed and said that it stunk and she'd never use it again." Jamie's eyes sparkled, and I knew he delighted in her discomfort.

"I'm not fond of those places myself." I sympathized with the woman and wondered what had gone through her mind when she discovered Walter's cabin wasn't exactly a five-star mountain retreat.

"Tell me about your night in the hut."

Jamie grew serious. "I was going to leave, but there was a storm and Scooter didn't want to go outside, so I stayed with him. I wouldn't desert my dog."

"I'm glad you didn't."

"There was a bed with a mattress, but in the night I had to keep getting up to put more wood on the fire. Scooter slept on the bed and kept me warm. Didn't you, boy?" Jamie rubbed behind the dog's ears and hugged him.

Scooter gave me a satisfied look, one that clearly stated, "I'm the hero of this story and I've won the battle to live here."

A few months ago, I would have replied with my own look, one that said, "No way, we're not having a dog in this house." Scooter was right though. He'd earned his stripes, and was a most welcome member of the family. I reached out, rubbed behind his ears, and smiled as he wiggled closer to me. He knew which side his bread was buttered on.

Jamie continued. "In the morning, Scooter kept whining to go out. I opened the door and he ran away."

I was thankful for the dog's sensitive hearing. "Garrett and I were calling your name. Scooter heard it, and came bounding down the mountain." I'd never been so glad to see a dog in my life. I reached across the table and took Jamie's hand.

"I have to ask you this question." I pushed away the pain that was wedged tight in my chest. "Do you want to go back with your dad?"

Jamie's answer was quick and sharp. "No. He doesn't want me. I want to stay with you."

Relieved and delighted, I stretched out my arms, and

said, "It's your choice. Now come and give me a hug."

Jamie jumped out of his chair and wrapped his arms around me. I marveled at his resilience. In the last six months, he'd been through so much. I had a new confidence in the child I'd been blessed with.

I kissed the top of his head and silently thanked Elena and Garrett, for their trust in me and for giving me such a precious gift.

Chapter Thirty-six

The doorbell rang as I ruffled Jamie's hair. He broke our hug and raced out of the room. I followed him.

Dottie flounced into the living room like a starlet who'd won the leading role in a new soap opera. Garrett trailed behind her, holding a large, flat package wrapped in brown paper.

I didn't have time to consider what he was carrying, because Dottie stopped and raised her hands. "Ta *daaa*!" She sang out the phrase like a messenger announcing the arrival of royalty. "We have a gift for you."

Garrett set the edge of the package on the floor and ripped away the paper, exposing my silk rug. It had been mounted in a beautiful, brown frame.

"Wow, neat." Jamie's eyes got bigger and rounder.

"I've always said that if you can't walk on a rug, you should stick it on the wall." Dottie marched to the end of the room. "This is where we'll hang it."

"Is that okay with you?" Garrett asked me.

"Everything's okay," I answered, wishing I could capture the moment forever—a moment when life was perfect.

Dottie pulled a tape measure out of her pocket and was checking out the wall. "If Rachel had any say in this matter, the rug would still be at the cleaners. We're the ones who rescued it and got it framed."

I wondered how I could have forgotten that I'd left it at the cleaners. I guess, in the interim, I'd realized that Jamie was more important.

"We'll center it here." Dottie marked the wall with a pencil.

Garrett got the needed tools, hammered in two nails, and in a few minutes, my rug filled the empty space on my wall.

"Do you like it, Scooter?" Jamie asked.

The dog thumped his tail against the hardwood and I stiffened, wondering if Scooter wanted to do an encore of his last visit to the living room.

He didn't.

The five of us stood back, admiring my newest piece of artwork. I had my arm around Jamie, and Garrett had one arm around me and the other around Dottie. Something caught in my throat, and I felt overwhelmed by all the love in the room. I had a son and two good friends. What more could a person want?

Dottie was first to break the silence. "I've made muffins and I'm inviting Jamie to be the first one to taste them, fresh out of the oven."

"Can Scooter come?" asked Jamie, his eyes lighting up.

"I think so." She winked at me. "We can have a long talk, while Rachel and Garrett stay and admire the artwork," she said, shrugging her shoulder and taking Jamie's hand, "or whatever." She nodded to Scooter. "Come along. There's food waiting for the three of us."

"What about Rachel and Garrett?" asked Jamie, as Dottie led him to the door, with Scooter following along behind.

"I'm sure they'll find something else to do." Dottie hustled him down the stairs, turned, and grinned as she made one last remark. "Don't do anything I wouldn't do."

Jamie giggled and then chanted, "I get it. Rachel's

gonna be all kissy face with Garrett."

Embarrassed, I quickly moved along behind them and closed the door, silencing Jamie's chatter. I let out a big sigh and turned around, smiling at Garrett, who had followed and stood close to me in the foyer. "Thank goodness that's ended."

"No, Rachel." Garrett took me into his arms. "Remember how I said I'd tell you when it was the right time?"

I felt my heart do a funny little jump in my chest. "Oh ... well, vaguely. So, is now the right time, do you think?"

He nodded, slowly and thoughtfully, staring down at me with a tender look in his eyes. "And believe me ... this is only the beginning."

Bringing Jamie Home Trilogy

Part Two

Jamie's Secret

(excerpt)

Chapter One

When I saw Walter Sorenson's name on my call display, I knew I didn't want to talk to him, but I knew I had to.

I put the phone on my nook table, pressed the talk button and said, "Good afternoon, Walter. What can I do for you?"

"Same old Rachel McGivney. Uptight as usual."

He paused, giving me time to think about his sarcastic words. Holding back my own cynical rebuttal, I gazed out the window into my back yard. The grass was still brown, but it'd start turning green in a few weeks.

"You shouldn't do it, Rachel."

"Do what?" I frowned at the phone.

"Adopt Jamie. We need to talk about it."

"I don't think there's anything to talk about. You gave

up your rights to your son, or have you changed your mind?" My harsh words masked the thumping of my heart. How could he be so cruel as to want Jamie back? He hadn't shown much interest in his son and now, after several months of being the child's guardian, I wanted to take the next step and adopt the ten-year-old boy whom I loved.

"I've been working on the necessary paperwork with Garrett Yates."

"Oh, yeah, your on-again off-again lawyer boyfriend. How is mister big shot?"

"Garrett is fine. As a courtesy, I sent the letter to let you know I'll be adopting Jamie. I didn't have to inform you."

"Yeah, yeah."

"Why did you phone?"

" Nobody's questioning your motives, Rachel, so you can stop apologizing. I'm phoning you today to warn you to stop the adoption."

"I don't know why you're pursuing this line of conversation. You know what my plans are, and I'm not going to change my mind no matter what you say." How could I make it any clearer to him?

"Whoa. Slow down."

He sounded like he was talking to a horse. I could picture Walter's pasty face and thinning hair. "It's time for Jamie to be in a real family. Someone who wants and loves him." I couldn't resist the extra jibe at the man who obviously didn't love his son.

"And I'm telling you, if you dig too deep, you won't like what you find."

Since the first time I'd met Walter, he'd annoyed me, and now he puzzled me. "What do you mean? Why don't you just tell me what's wrong?"

"It's not simple. There's lots you don't know."

Walter's words startled me and at the same time frightened me. "What don't I know?"

"It's a long story, Rachel."

I glanced outside. The flower bed running below the stone fence was ready for bedding-out plants once the weather warmed up. My low spreading junipers appeared to have survived the winter, ready for the red geraniums I'd plant at the end of this month or in early June.

Anxious to get back to my own work, I said, "Why don't you explain the big secret?"

"It's not easy. I need to talk to you and…" he lowered his voice, "not over the phone."

Although Walter had never been to my house before and knowing I'd never settle until he told me the "secret," I relented, "Come over and we'll talk." I gave him the address and then hung up.

I didn't have to wait long. Within fifteen minutes, as I gazed out my living room window, a black sedan crawled down the street. The driver stopped on the opposite side and seemed to be checking out my house.

He got out of the car and crossed the road. My knees wobbled and I braced my hands against the window sill. Walter Sorenson and good news were never in the same neighborhood. Walter gave up any legal rights to Jamie two years ago when he divorced Jamie's mom. She'd died last fall and I'd become Jamie's guardian.

Although it wasn't legally accurate, I called him my son.

I greeted Walter through the screen as he climbed the steps. "Good afternoon."

In my opinion the day promised to be anything but good.

He paused. "How ya doing, Rachel?"

I wanted to tell him that until his phone call, I was on top of the world, instead I decided to keep quiet and listen.

"I'm fine, thank you," I lied.

Since I'd last seen Walter he'd grown a handlebar mustache and his sandy hair appeared sparser. The few extra pounds he'd gained showed on his cheeks. His head reminded me of a pink billiard ball with a felt-penned face and his cynical expression made me think he had bad news he'd love to share with me.

I opened the outside door. "Come in."

"Don't mind if I do."

Moving backwards into the living room, I gave Walter plenty of space in the tiny entrance hall. He took off his jacket and tossed it on the sofa, like he owned the place. The coins in his pocket jingled and his pants were baggy, with bulging pockets.

"Have a seat?" I indicated the living room, hoping he didn't notice my polite words masked my anxiety. He made himself comfortable and rested his arm on the sofa that separated the living room from the dining room.

I sat on the opposite side, in one of my wingback chairs with my hands tucked under my legs, so they wouldn't shake.

"How's Jamie?" he asked.

I tried to sound nonchalant. "Fine."

"How's the kid doin' at school?"

"Very well. He's bright and eager and enjoys fifth grade." I didn't know why I was praising his virtues. Walter never questioned his son's intelligence.

"Yeah, I always wondered where the kid got his smarts, certainly not from me."

I couldn't have agreed more.

Walter sneered. "He didn't get them from Elena either."

Walter hadn't changed from the last time I'd met him and it didn't take more than a few minutes for him to annoy me.

"Elena Sorenson was a wonderful mom. She doted on Jamie," I said.

He gave an indifferent shrug and rolled his eyes. "A real schemer."

As usual, Walter pressed my buttons and before I

realized it, I was standing in front of him and shaking my finger in his face. "In my house I won't have you discussing your ex-wife and Jamie's mother in such a disrespectful manner."

Walter waved his hand, dismissing my comment. "I didn't bother coming all this way to yak about my dead ex-wife."

I cringed at his callous words. "Show some respect." Taking a deep breath, I willed myself to be calm. Letting Walter Sorenson get the better of me wouldn't help. I backed up and sat, voicing the one question playing in my mind.

"What is the secret that you couldn't tell me on the phone?"

He twisted, reached inside his jacket pocket and pulled out an envelope, revealing the letter I'd mailed. Walter dropped it on the coffee table. He leaned forward, lines etching his face. "Why are you doing this?"

I waved my hand at the letter. "It's all explained in there. Soon I'll be making application to legally adopt Jamie and I wanted to let you know."

He shook his head. "Like I told you. Not a good idea."

Warning bells went off in my head. Fearing he wanted Jamie back, I held my head high, determined to appear confident. "I won't give Jamie up without a fight. I love him and he's happy living with me. Garrett loves him."

Walter flicked his wrist, as if I were some sort of aggravating housefly. "I'm not here to discuss your lover boy." He smirked and his upper lip curled. "You're a tight-ass so I'd guess you're fussing over the kid and he's probably fine."

I cringed and bit my tongue, determined not to let Walter know how his language offended me and his whole manner antagonized me. Okay. I was a little uptight, but I didn't need to have the fact shoved in my face. I only wanted the best for Jamie, unlike Walter, who was lounging on the sofa, his fingers clasped, while he rotated his thumbs.

After an agonizing few minutes, he stopped and gazed at me. "I didn't like your hoity-toity, butter-wouldn't-melt-in-your-mouth attitude the first time I met you. I saw you snicker at my lady friend."

I hadn't snickered at his female companion because I'd been too busy gritting my teeth. I've been told my face is an open book and I imagined what Walter read on it right now was disgust and annoyance. I'd met the voluptuous Delilah, last December, and I wasn't impressed. In my opinion she didn't care about Jamie. This past winter Jamie had run away from them. The two lovebirds weren't concerned about his disappearance until Garrett and I arrived on the scene.

I guess I wanted Walter's okay for the adoption, maybe even his blessings. It'd seemed reasonable. Maybe, I secretly wished he'd shown some love or interest in his only son. When I was seven my stepfather had deserted the family and I'd longed for him to come back home.

He never did.

Walter hadn't interfered with my plans. I guess I should have been thankful, but his indifference annoyed me.

"Please tell me why you're here." I sounded haughty, but Walter and I had rubbed each other the wrong way from the first time we met.

He snorted. "I wasn't going to tell you, but you accused me of being a bad father. It's not true. I told you all those doting father and son pictures of me and Jamie was nothing but a big lie. Elena always pretended we were the perfect family. We weren't." His mouth formed a determined line.

I couldn't let him think he'd gotten the better of Elena. "Of course not. You were divorced; I certainly didn't expect you to have warm feelings for her. However, I expected something better for Jamie." I remembered Walter's comments last winter. He'd said Elena insisted on photos of father and son and, at the time, I'd believed he was exaggerating.

Walter's upper lip curled like a snarling dog's. "You don't know half as much as you think you do. You hated me so much you didn't see the truth."

"And the point is…" The faster he left the house, the better.

A smirk twisted his lips. "The point is. I don't care about Jamie, because I'm not his father."

I gripped the arm of the chair. Open-mouthed, I gaped and then sucked in air.

After seconds of stunned silence I said, "What do you mean?"

Was this his idea of payback to see how upset I'd get?

Walter grabbed his jacket and walked to the front door. I followed, trying to grab his arm—hoping to make him stay. "Who is the father? You have to tell me."

He pushed my hand away. "Listen lady, I don't have to tell you anything. I wanted to get you off my back."

I shook my head. "I thought you'd be interested in the adoption."

Walter scowled. "You should have left well enough alone."

"Jus' keep your mouth shut." His lips tightened.

I fisted my hand and pressed it against my mouth, preventing myself from saying something I'd later regret.

"Like I told you, the kid and I aren't related.

"Then who is the father?"

Walter shoved his arm into his jacket sleeve. "Beats me."

"I thought you and Elena were married…before Jamie was born."

"We were and then Jamie appeared. See lady, you didn't know diddly-squat about Elena." He jerked his head back and once again snorted. "She wasn't the goody two-shoes you made her out to be."

I drew my own conclusion. When Walter and Elena were married, she must have had an affair with another man, and the resentful Walter could never love Jamie as his own son. I should have noticed it before. Jamie's brown hair showed a reddish color in the sunlight, not at all like Walter's.

And Elena? Did Jamie resemble her? I couldn't tell. In the last few months before she died, she'd been so sick. Who would have seen any likeness to a healthy ten-year-old boy?

Shocked at his revelation, I pressed my fingers against my chin while my insides churned.

Once outside, he turned and gave me one last verbal sting. "Don't go nosing around. You might not like what you find."

As he hurried down the stairs, I called, "Please, come back. You've got to tell me."

Walter jerked a thumb over one shoulder and shrugged me off. "I don't know anything about him. I'm warning you for the last time. Leave well enough alone."

He carried on down the sidewalk and then turned and took a few steps toward me. "Promise me you'll tell Garrett to stop the adoption and you'll forget it."

The sickening lump in my stomach rose to my chest. I'd make no such vow, so I said, "I'll think about it and let you know."

He turned around and got into his car. Tires squealed as he drove away.

I staggered into the living room, flopped on the sofa and rested my head against my hands, my body shaking.

Was Walter implying that Jamie's father might reappear and demand custody? I wouldn't let it happen, however, now I understood Walter's cold and indifferent attitude. No matter how uninterested he'd acted toward Jamie, I'd still prefer Walter to be Jamie's biological father, rather than some nameless man.

Dear Reader,

Please visit my website at www.SherileReilly.com where you can see Rachel's geraniums. There is also a photo of Scooter.

If you enjoyed Jamie's Choice
you can help others find this story
by leaving a short review on Amazon.

Thanks!
Sherile Reilly

Bringing Jamie Home Trilogy:
Jamie's Choice
Jamie's Secret
Jamie's Gift

About the Author

A former school teacher, Sherile Reilly writes Clean Contemporary Romance, Gothic Paranormal Romance and Middle Readers—books for kids of all ages. Quite a variety!

www.SherileReilly.com